REST

in

PEACE

REST

in

PEACE

Frances Devine

BARBOUR
PUBLISHING

Cover design: Faceout Studio, www.faceoutstudio.com

Published by Barbour Publishing, Inc., P.O. Box 719, Uhrichsville, OH 44683, www.barbourbooks.com

Our mission is to publish and distribute inspirational products offering exceptional value and biblical encouragement to the masses.

 Member of the
Evangelical Christian
Publishers Association

Printed in the United States of America.

DEDICATION

I'd like to thank Susan Downs, who was willing to take a chance on *The Misadventures of Miss Aggie*, and Barbour Publishing for their helping hand to new authors. To Nancy Toback, whose editing skills helped to get the manuscript to its final form in the best shape possible. Thanks, Nancy.

Thanks to Cedric Benoit for being kind enough to allow me to put him and his wonderful band, The Cajun Connection, into my stories. You're the greatest.

To Silver Dollar City for giving me permission to mention you in all three books.

To my friends at the Hughes Senior Center who pray for me.

To Carol, who tells me to write and then prays that God will inspire me.

To my family. You are all my darling angels.

And to my heavenly Father, thank You for giving me the desires of my heart.

FRANCES L. DEVINE grew up in the great state of Texas, where she wrote her first story at the age of nine. She moved to southwest Missouri more than twenty years ago and fell in love with the hills, the fall colors, and Silver Dollar City. Frances has always loved to read, especially cozy mysteries, and considers herself blessed to have the opportunity to write in her favorite genre. She is the mother of seven adult children and has fourteen wonderful grandchildren. Frances is happy to hear from her fans. Please e-mail her at cozymysteries@aol.com.

CHAPTER ONE

"Come—*umph*—on—Buster!" I pulled and tugged in an attempt to get the monster of a dog out of the backseat of the van. Apparently he remembered Clyde Foster's pet store all too well. *Sorry old boy, shot time again.*

I wasn't entirely sure it was legal for Clyde to be giving shots, but the seniors at Cedar Lodge Boarding House assured me he'd been doing it for years, and the alternative was a thirty-mile drive down curving roads to Branson. One final tug and the unwilling animal came sliding off the seat. Sighing with relief, I blew a stray lock of hair from my forehead, snapped the leash onto Buster's collar, and headed for the door. I didn't always win these wrestling matches with the humongous dog.

As we approached the shop, Buster stopped abruptly. His hair bristled, and a low growl emitted from his throat.

"What's wrong, boy? Smell a cat in there?" I reached for the doorknob.

Buster stared up at me and whined, blocking the door.

Dread washed over me. A feeling I had become familiar with in the past couple of years. This was more than Buster's reluctance to get a shot.

"It's okay, boy. Let's take a look inside." I turned the knob, then with caution, pushed the door open. Buster pressed close against me as I stepped inside. A loud screech pierced the air. I screamed and pressed my hand to my thundering heart. Catching my breath, I forced a chuckle. Clyde's parrot, Whatzit, was going to be the death of someone one of these days. Still, it wasn't like him to screech so long and loud. I glanced toward his cage, surprised to find it empty.

Sunlight streamed in through the open door, flooding the room with daylight. The overhead light still burned, as well as several wall lights. Highly unusual. Clyde was known for being very frugal, or cheap, as some would say. His customers often complained that he kept the shop too dark.

"Mr. Foster?" My voice cracked. I really needed to get a grip. For crying out loud, I was thirty-one, not ten. I cleared my throat and tried again. "Mr. Foster, it's me, Victoria Storm. I have Buster with me for his shot."

A heavy silence lay on the shop. I drew a deep breath. *Get yourself together, silly. He probably went upstairs for something.* But Buster had started toward the rear of the shop, a low growl coming once more from his throat.

I followed cautiously through the door into the dark storage area.

"Mr. Foster?" My strained whisper seemed loud in the dead silence, but Clyde Foster either didn't hear or chose not to answer.

Swallowing hard, I blinked, and suddenly my eyes became accustomed to the darkness. I gasped and froze in my tracks. Nausea washed over me. Clyde lay sprawled on the floor, halfway on his stomach, his head sideways in a pool of blood.

Buster stood beside him, whining as he nudged the still form.

I forced myself to move, stumbled across the room. Bending, I pressed two fingers against his throat. No pulse.

With shaking hands, I yanked my cell phone from the front pocket of my jeans and dialed 911. After telling the dispatcher what I'd found, I pulled on Buster's leash and stumbled back into the front room of the shop. Whatzit was perched on a corner of a supply cabinet and continued his ear-splitting screech.

"It's okay, Whatzit. It's okay." My voice trembled as I tried to calm him. Wild-eyed, he stared at me and then began to squawk unintelligibly again.

Poor Whatzit. Of course it wasn't okay. And apparently, he knew that very well. I approached him warily. Should I try to get him back into his cage? Not with that look in his eyes. I headed toward the door, and Buster growled at the bird before following me.

I peered out the door, watching for the sheriff. What in the world would Whatzit do now? Who'd want to take the cantankerous bird? Miss Aggie, maybe. I took a deep breath. What was wrong with me? Worrying about a bird when a man was dead? Okay, so Clyde was mean and crabby and had scared me half to death when I was a child. But as far as I knew, he was all alone. If he had family, I'd never heard of them.

I sighed with relief as the sheriff's vehicle turned the corner and pulled up in front of the pet shop. Sheriff Bob Turner and his deputy, Tom Lewis, got out and headed toward the door.

When the sheriff saw me, he stopped in his tracks and frowned.

"Victoria, are you the one who called about a body?"

"Yes." I was happy the word came out strong. I wouldn't want Bob Turner to have the satisfaction of knowing how shook-up I was. "Mr. Foster's in the back room, and I think. . .he's dead."

He grunted and walked past me with Tom Lewis tailing him like a shadow. Like the sheriff's little puppy. *Ah. Stop that, Victoria.* Sarcasm seemed to be second nature with me, but I'd been doing so much better lately. Well, except in my thoughts. *Sorry, Lord.*

I hurried after the two officers.

The sheriff stooped down next to Clyde and checked for a pulse. "Tom, get the coroner over here. He's dead all right. Looks like he fell and hit his head on that stone doorstop."

I glanced at the doorstop and could make out a dark blotch. Nausea threatened to rise up again. I swallowed and licked my dry lips.

The sheriff stood, rubbing his back, then turned and scowled as he saw me standing by the door.

"Don't look at me like that. I didn't kill him." My voice sounded guilty to my own ears.

"Did anyone say you did?"

The sheriff and I had a cautious respect for one another, but I suspected he didn't like me very much. For the life of me, I couldn't figure out why. Did he think it was my fault I kept getting mixed-up in what he considered his business? I certainly didn't get involved with kidnappers and dead bodies on purpose.

After asking a few questions, he told me I could leave.

"Do you have a problem with me taking Whatzit with

me? Miss Aggie might be able to calm him down. He's used to her."

He scratched his head. "I guess it's okay. One less animal I have to worry about." He glanced at the snake cage, and his face paled. I couldn't help grinning. I'd bet he wouldn't be the one to care for the other pets in the store. "But only until we can get in touch with Clyde's next of kin," he added.

Skirting Clyde's body, I made my way over to the corner of the room and grabbed Whatzit's heavy portable cage, then wrestled it into the front room. After a little coaxing, Whatzit hopped into it. Tom carried it to the van for me and placed it on the backseat, while I opened the passenger door for Buster to get in. I drove home as Whatzit's insane screeching and Buster's furious barking knifed through my skull. I turned onto my street, and Cedar Lodge Boarding House came into view. Fallen leaves scattered about, promising an early fall. Ivy grew up the bricks of both front-wall fireplaces, lending ambience to the centuries-old ex-hunting lodge. Pulling into the wide driveway, I drove into the parking garage. Then reality hit me. How would my senior boarders and friends take the news of Mr. Foster's death? None of them were close to him, except Miss Aggie, but they'd known him for years. Besides, they'd been through so much over the past two years with Miss Aggie's kidnapping and then the murder at Pennington House.

I managed to get Whatzit's cage off the backseat and onto a worktable in the rear of the garage. When I opened the van door, Buster sprang out and jumped on me, his huge front paws landing on my chest.

"Calm down, old boy. And let's not spill the beans just

yet." I rubbed his head, grabbed his leash, and headed for the side door. I'd wait until they were all together to break the news gently. It's hard to hear about a neighbor dying, and all alone, at that.

I inhaled deeply. The spicy aroma wafting from the spick-and-span kitchen washed over me like liquid peace. I unclipped the leash from Buster's collar, and he shot out into the hall and headed to the recreation room. I didn't blame him. He knew where love and safety lay. By the time I got there, he was reveling in the adoration of Miss Jane and Miss Georgina. Martin Downey looked on with an impatient frown.

"Victoria, come join us. We were just about to start a game of dominoes." Miss Jane Brody motioned from the card table.

"You just want me to play because you and Miss Georgina always beat me," I teased.

"Why, Victoria Storm, that's not true. We love your company." Miss Georgina twisted her hankie and gave me a worried look.

"I know, Miss Georgina. I was joking." I walked over and kissed the sweet lady on her plump face, then glanced around the room. "Where's Miss Aggie?"

"Where do you think?" Miss Jane grinned, and her thin face lit up. "Putting finishing touches, as she calls it, on Pennington House. She's so excited, I think she might explode before opening day."

I knew what she meant. Since Miss Aggie Pennington-Brown and her nephew Dane, who we called Corky, started renovations on the family mansion, Miss Aggie hardly stayed still a moment. The grand opening of the swanky hotel and restaurant was scheduled for November 1st, just a couple of months away. A first of its kind for Cedar Chapel. But its proximity to Branson and the Lake of the Ozarks should be favorable for business. Miss Aggie couldn't wait to move into her new apartment in her girlhood home.

"Did she say if she'd be home for lunch?" I didn't want to have to repeat the sad news twice.

"Yeah." Martin snorted. "She's going to eat lunch, then drive to Branson to spend more money on fancy gewgaws."

"How about Miss Evalina and Frank?" Evalina Swayne and Frank Cordell, who had been childhood sweethearts before Frank fell for someone else, had surprised us all by announcing their engagement the year before. They'd been married just before Christmas here at the lodge. We'd all expected them to move into their own home since Frank was very well-off due to a percentage from the candy stores he'd turned over to his son. But to our surprise and delight they'd chosen to remain among their old friends. They now resided in the elaborate second-floor suite vacated by former actress and their old acquaintance, Jeannette Simone.

"Eva and Frank are shopping. Should be home any minute," Miss Jane informed me.

Good. I'd only have to break the news to them once, while the group was together after lunch. That is, if Miss Evalina and Mr. Frank didn't hear about it while they were out.

The house phone rang, and I hurried into the hall and snatched it from its cradle. "Hello?"

"Victoria, Bob Turner here." The sheriff's voice was clipped. "The coroner has ruled Clyde Foster's death an accident, just as I said it was. I wanted to let you know we don't need more information from you."

Puzzled, I thanked him and hung up. Why would he bother to call just to tell me he *didn't* need anything? Did he simply want me to know he was right about the death being an accident? Rather odd. I shrugged and went back into the rec room.

CB

Unusual silence hung over us as we sat in the front parlor. I'd told them about Clyde's death. After the initial cries of dismay, the seniors had grown quiet. Miss Aggie had taken Whatzit up to her room, and the other seniors had gathered in the rec room. When I'd peeked in an hour or so later and heard the sighs of discontent, I asked them all to come into the parlor for tea. I wished someone would say something. Even Buster, stretched out in front of the empty corner fireplace, lay unusually still.

Finally, Frank cleared his throat. "Are they sure it was an accident?"

A rustling sound spread throughout the room as the rest of the gang seemed to come to attention. Six expectant faces turned my way.

"That's what the sheriff told me." Maybe my voice didn't sound too certain. The expressions across my friends' faces ranged from vague worry to dread.

"I don't know why he'd lie to me." Oops. That sounded even worse.

"Victoria, what are you keeping from us?" Miss Evalina's intense gaze told me she'd stand for no nonsense. I wondered how many children had folded under that look through the years. Even now, the retired teacher could send quivers through me.

"Nothing, Miss Evalina, I promise. It was just a vague feeling I had when I saw the body."

When they continued to stare, I told them about Bob Turner phoning me for no apparent reason. There, that was all I knew. I hoped it would be enough for them.

Miss Evalina nodded, apparently satisfied. "Makes sense. Bob probably forgot to tell you he might need to talk to you some more. And vague feelings can be caused by indigestion. With a grand opening and two weddings coming up in a few months, we don't have time for another mystery."

Butterflies danced in my tummy as I thought of Benjamin, my fiancé. We were planning our wedding for Christmas Eve at Pennington House. Corky and Phoebe's wedding, scheduled for the week before ours, would actually be the first one to take place at the newly renovated mansion. And that was only right. After all, Corky was a Pennington.

"I'm not so sure." Miss Aggie spoke up from the wing chair by the door.

"What do you mean, Aggie?"

Excitement darted from Miss Aggie's eyes. "I know what Whatzit is screaming about." She paused and glanced around. "I didn't think much of it, but if there's any question about Clyde's death being an accident, it could be important."

"What is it, Aggie?" Martin hated what he viewed as melodrama. "Are you going to tell us or not?"

"Oh, don't be so snappy. I was getting ready to tell you. He's saying, 'No, no, get out!'"

To be honest, the fake fear in her voice gave me a chill.

Maybe Miss Aggie had taken a few acting lessons from Miss Simone. Or was it possible Miss Aggie really was afraid?

"I don't remember hearing him say that before." Miss Georgina's voice shook, and I knew I'd better do something before she went into hysterics.

"Of course you didn't," Miss Aggie said. "He's repeating what Clyde said to his killer."

I sidled over to the other end of the sofa and took Miss Georgina's hand. *Oh Lord, please don't let her faint.*

Miss Evalina rose, fury on her face. "Aggie Brown, stop it right now. You're upsetting Georgina." She turned to her cousin. "Don't pay any mind to her. She's just trying to get attention, as usual."

"I was merely telling you what the stupid parrot was saying," Miss Aggie snapped, her eyes flashing. "Don't be such a scaredy-cat, Georgina. We're in our own parlor, for goodness sake. Do you think Victoria would let anyone hurt you?"

For the first time since inheriting Grandma's house, I was having unkind thoughts about one of her old friends. Actually, I felt like shaking Miss Aggie.

"Dang, Aggie, don't be so mean." Martin, who usually had little patience for Miss Georgina's timidity, was actually coming to her defense. Or maybe his dislike for Miss Aggie was stronger.

Feeling a bit guilty for my own irritation, I figured I'd better take control of the situation.

"Okay, folks. We're all upset, and our nerves are on edge. We need to calm down and stop fighting among ourselves."

"Maybe Aggie's right." Frank sent an apologetic glance in his wife's direction. "It's something to think about anyway."

"I've been thinking the same thing." Miss Jane spoke up for the first time. "Of course, she shouldn't have spoken so harshly to you, dear." She cast a gentle smile at Miss Georgina.

The doorbell rang, and I hurried to the front door to find Benjamin standing with a gallon of ice cream in his hand and a tender smile on his face.

"You've heard the news," I said.

"Yep. Thought you and the seniors might need cheering up."

I took the ice cream to the freezer, then went back to the parlor with Benjamin. I had to think of a way to keep the seniors from telling Ben their suspicions. As owner of the *Cedar Chapel Gazette*, Ben was always nosing around for anything out of the ordinary. And I had a hunch he wouldn't take it too well if he thought we were getting mixed-up in another crime. Not that I wanted to keep anything from him, but why spread rumors based on Miss Aggie's imagination— and mine?

"Benjamin, you're here just in time. Did you hear about Clyde's murder?" *No, no, Miss Aggie.*

I groaned as Ben tossed an accusing glance in my direction. "Murder? I heard it was an accident."

"I'm sure it is," I said, shooting a warning look at Miss Aggie. "We have no evidence to the contrary."

"Humph." She wasn't going to let it be. "Maybe not evidence, but I'd say a parrot screaming 'No, no, get out' is pretty suspicious."

"What's this about, Vickie? I should have known you were up to something when your eyes turned from hazel to green."

I frowned, but now that Miss Aggie had let the cat out of the bag, I told Ben everything.

"Hmm. That's not much to base suspicion of murder on."

"I know. That's what I tried to tell you."

"Still, I don't think I've ever heard Whatzit say those words either." He frowned. "Tell me again what Bob Turner said when he called."

I repeated the sheriff's words as closely as I could remember.

"It does almost sound as though he was trying to throw you off the trail, but maybe he was just being thoughtful."

At my rueful expression, he laughed. "Yeah, thoughtful doesn't sound like Bob."

"Not to me anyway. Sometimes I think he hates me."

"Now, you know he doesn't hate you." Dear Miss Georgina, always trying to think the best of everyone.

"He may not hate her, but he doesn't especially like the way she solves his cases before he does." Miss Jane had become my champion lately, and it felt good.

I laughed and gave her a hug. "To be fair, Sheriff Turner does a great job of keeping our town fairly crime free. I was just lucky a couple of times."

"You know what we need?" Miss Georgina's face was awash with excitement. "We all need to take a trip to Silver Dollar City to get our minds off things."

"Oh sure, Georgina. We all know your reason for wanting to go to that theme park." Miss Jane teased her friend relentlessly about the crush she had on the good-looking leader of The Cajun Connection, one of the bands at Silver Dollar City.

Miss Georgina's face flamed. "Now you stop that. He's

young enough to be my son. I just like his music, is all."

Relieved to see them moving on to another subject, I thought I'd add my two cents. "I think Silver Dollar City is a great idea. Isn't the autumn festival going on now?"

"Yes!" Miss Georgina punched the air with her fisted hand.

I sat back and relaxed as friendly laughter rang through the room. We might have our differences sometimes, but these seniors were family to me—all the family I really had since my grandparents went to be with Jesus. A familiar twinge clutched at me. I drew a breath and shoved away the hurtful past. Mom and Dad had never been family to me, and it was doubtful they ever would be.

"Victoria, stop daydreaming." Miss Jane tossed a ball of yarn at me, which Buster quickly intercepted. "We were just saying it would be nice to have the wedding at Wilderness Church at the park."

I laughed at her teasing tone. The quaint, rustic church was truly wonderful, and people did get married there. But Miss Jane knew I'd been dreaming of a Pennington House wedding.

I just hoped nothing was going to disrupt that dream.

CHAPTER ⛢ TWO

"Poor Whatzit," Miss Aggie said on a sigh as she stepped into my office.

I looked up from my account book. The information needed to be entered into my computer, but who had time with everything going on?

"What's wrong with Whatzit? Not sick, is he?"

"Oh no, no. He's healthy enough. But I hate seeing him cooped up in that portable cage. Couldn't we bring the other one over?"

I tapped my pen on the desk. "Not a bad idea. It gives us an excuse to go to the pet store. If the sheriff doesn't consider it a crime scene, perhaps he hasn't searched it. But how do we get in?"

"Oh, I have a key. You know I looked after Whatzit whenever Clyde was out of town."

How well I knew. Once she'd even managed to sneak the cantankerous parrot into her room overnight. I never did figure out how she kept him from making a sound.

"Okay. Let me finish up here."

"Good, I'll ask Martin to go along to help with the cage."

An hour later, after Martin and Frank had carried the

cage out to the van, the four of us spread out around the pet shop.

Someone had obviously been in to care for the animals. The cages were clean, and water and food containers had been filled.

"What exactly are we looking for?" Frowning, Frank scratched his head.

"Anything out of the ordinary," I said absently as I searched though a supply cabinet.

"But how do we know if something wasn't ordinary? Clyde wasn't exactly the most outgoing person, you know."

"Yeah!" Martin chimed in. "Maybe he was a CIA agent or something." He snickered sarcastically.

Miss Aggie glared at the men. "If you two aren't going to help, you might as well leave. Victoria and I can handle this nicely."

"Naw, we'll help." Martin grinned and followed Frank toward the back room.

I headed upstairs. Maybe Clyde's living quarters would be a more logical place to search.

The small kitchenette-style apartment was dark and dreary. I wished I could raise a window, but if Bob Turner got wind of what we were doing, he'd be furious.

A small corner desk caught my eye, and I felt a surge of excitement. I rummaged through drawers, searching every corner with eyes and fingers. I pounced on a ledger in the center drawer and skimmed through the pages. Nothing. Disappointed, I turned away and approached the four-poster.

"Hey! I found something." Martin's shout sent me

rushing down the stairs and into the back room, where he stood gazing at a large box.

"What is it?" I managed to gasp out.

"Look, W. C. Fields." He held the box so I could see inside.

I was going to kill that man. Him and his obsession with the red-nosed actor from the thirties.

"Martin," I said, as calmly as possible through clenched teeth. "Clyde's movie collection isn't what I had in mind."

"Sorry," he mumbled, a sheepish look on his face. "I just got excited when I saw them."

Nothing had been found downstairs, so Miss Aggie followed me up to the living quarters while Frank and Martin went to the van.

"I don't think we're going to find anything, Miss Aggie. I've pretty much covered the whole apartment."

She sighed. "It was a long shot."

"I was just getting ready to check the bed and dresser." I began to go through dresser drawers.

"Victoria. . ."

I whirled at Miss Aggie's whisper.

She stood beside the bed with a round, wooden knob from one of the bedposts in one hand. A peculiar look was on her face.

"Did you find something?"

She held out a fragment of paper, and I took it. All that I could make out were the letters *n-n-e-l*.

"I don't understand. It's just a piece of torn paper."

"I remembered how my friends and I used to hide things in the bedpost knobs when we were children, so I looked inside this one. This fragment must have torn off when someone removed whatever was in there."

"But what do you think it is?"

"I'm not sure, but the letters could very well be part of the word 'tunnel.'"

"But. . ." I stopped, suddenly realizing what was going through her head. "Do you think this is referring to one of the secret tunnels at Pennington House?" *Not so secret anymore.*

She looked at me with an ashen face.

"Doesn't every evil event lead back to my old home?" Her voice sounded strangled. So rare for the self-assured ex-debutante.

I put my arm around her shoulders. "Now Miss Aggie, even if the word is *tunnel*, it could mean something quite innocent."

"No." The word came out hard and insistent. "Clyde Foster was involved in something illegal going on at Pennington. Just as my brother, Forrest, and my husband were. I've always suspected it of those two."

"But, if it's true, why would someone kill Clyde now? The criminal activity, whatever it was, must have taken place years ago."

"I don't know. Maybe it has something to do with the emeralds."

I didn't want to admit it, but it did make sense. The Pennington emeralds had disappeared years ago and had never been found. Miss Aggie didn't even know where they had originally come from.

I tucked the fragment in my jeans pocket and took one last look around the room before we left.

When we got back to the lodge, Miss Jane and Miss Georgina had gone to the senior center to play bingo, so we agreed to share our find with them after dinner. Miss Aggie went upstairs to rest, but the aroma of roasting chicken guided my steps to the kitchen. Mabel, our wonderful cook, stood placing sweet potatoes on a baking pan. She'd been with us for a year now, and it was a relief not to worry about meals.

"Ummm, what's for dinner? I'm starving."

"Chicken and dumplings." Mabel huffed out a breath. "That's if people stop parading through the kitchen every five minutes."

I stared at her. I'd never seen her so testy before.

Noticing my confusion, she wiped her hands on her apron and looked me in the eye. "I'm afraid I'm going to have to leave. And I can't even give my two weeks' notice."

I groaned. Why couldn't I keep a cook? "But why? Don't you like it here?"

"Of course I do." Suddenly, her face crumpled. She reached up and wiped the corner of her eye. "I like it here better than anyplace I've worked, but my granddaughter, Sarah, is coming to live with me."

"Your granddaughter?" I knew her oldest son had a young daughter, but why would she come to live with Mabel?

"Yeah. Bobby's wife, Carol, walked out on him and their daughter, Sarah, last week. They ain't heard hide nor hair of her since. Bobby can't work and take care of Sarah."

"She's not an infant, is she?"

"Nah. She's ten, but she's a corker. He don't dare leave her alone after school." Mabel took a handkerchief from her apron pocket and wiped her eyes.

"Oh. I'm sorry to hear the news."

She sniffed and turned back to her task. "Anyway, at least you have Jane to help out until you can find someone."

That was true. Miss Jane was an excellent cook, and she loved it when she could prepare the meals. Still, it wouldn't be easy to find another good cook like Mabel. We'd all gotten rather spoiled when Corky was cooking for us. Of course we didn't know at that time that he was practically a master chef. Mabel had filled his shoes nicely.

I knew I should probably think this over, but I wasn't about to lose Mabel if I could help it. "How about bringing her with you? On school days she can catch the bus here and then get off here after school. The bus stops at the corner. I know. The monsters across the street ride it."

Mabel's mouth dropped open, and hope flickered in her eyes. "Are you sure? The girl can be a handful. What about the old people?"

"Oh phooey. What sort of trouble could a ten-year-old girl cause? I'm sure the seniors will love having a child around." I hoped so anyway. "When is she coming?"

"In a couple of weeks. Bobby figures he needs to keep her until she adjusts a little more to her mama being gone." Mabel shook her head. "It would be an answer to prayer, if you're sure."

"Then it's settled. I can't wait to meet Sarah." Happy and a bit smug to have resolved the matter, I went into my office to work on the accounts.

I sighed as I sat behind my desk. What had I done? The peace and normalcy had been nice while it lasted.

०४

The temperature had been dropping since midafternoon, so I built a small fire in the front parlor. The first of the season. I hoped it would cheer up all of us. Miss Aggie had called Corky and asked him to come over, and I'd contacted Ben. I suspected I might need help in keeping imaginations from running wild. Things were bad enough as it was. Benjamin was extremely level-headed—sometimes he was too level-headed, but that's what I needed tonight.

The comforting warmth and spicy aroma of tea and cookies should help, too. I breathed a silent thank-you to Mabel, who'd made the cookies before she went home.

Benjamin and I sat on either side of a small table directly across from the corner fireplace. Corky and Phoebe shared a love seat, and the seniors sat on the two sofas. The curtains at the front window were open, and darkness outside gave an eerie feeling to the room. I shivered. Miss Aggie must have had the same feeling because she got up, closed the curtains, and switched on the light.

"All right. Does someone want to tell me what's going on?" Straight and to the point. That's Benjamin. I figured I'd do likewise.

"We went to the pet store today, and while we were there, we found something." I handed him the fragment.

Benjamin stared at the fragment, a frown creasing his forehead. "Okay, what is it?"

"Here, let me see." Frank reached over, and Benjamin handed him the piece of paper. As it was passed to Corky and Martin, they each wore the same puzzled expression as Ben.

Georgina looked at the note and gasped, her face going

white. She handed it to Miss Jane.

"Tunnels. It's about the tunnels at Pennington House." Miss Jane's voice was filled with excitement.

"Here, let me see that again." Frank perused the fragment and nodded, handing it to Miss Evalina. "Could be. What do you think, Evie?"

"It's a possibility." She frowned. "In fact, I'd say the letters are definitely part of the word 'tunnel,' but we shouldn't assume it to be a reference to Pennington." She handed the paper to me, and this time I placed it in a small, decorative box on the mantel.

"But it is. I know it is." Miss Aggie bit her lip and tapped her fingers on the side table.

I could feel myself getting carried away by her agitation. I inhaled deeply, then slowly exhaled.

Corky got up and went over to his aunt. He stooped down beside her and took her hand. "Aunt Aggie, don't you think there's a possibility you're building this up in your head a bit?"

I cringed. *Bad tactic, Corky*.

Miss Aggie jerked her hand from her nephew's and glared. "I'm not senile yet, Dane Pennington. And I'll thank you to remember that."

Corky flinched. "Sorry, Aunt Aggie. Of course I don't think you're senile." He stood and returned to his seat beside Phoebe, who patted his hand and smiled sympathetically.

"No one thinks you're senile, Miss Aggie." Benjamin smiled her way. "I'm sure you have good reason for believing Clyde may have been mixed up in shady dealings at Pennington."

I couldn't help wondering what that reason could be. I knew Miss Aggie and Clyde were friends, but wouldn't he have been too young to be involved with Forrest Pennington when he was on the scene?

"Miss Aggie, wouldn't Clyde have been a boy when the emeralds disappeared?"

She sighed. "A little more than that. He was nineteen, I believe. He had a hero worship of Forrest, who rescued him from a bad situation when he was a small child. Every time my brother came home for a visit, Clyde trailed him like a puppy. I can see how easily he could have been influenced."

"I see. It does seem suspicious." I glanced at Benjamin, who was nodding. "Okay, so we need to decide our next step."

"That's easy. Take the piece of paper to Bob Turner." Benjamin looked at me intently, obviously expecting an argument.

Miss Jane beat me to it. "He'll just laugh at us like he always does."

Martin snorted. "He didn't just laugh. He was downright rude to us."

"But if the note is evidence. . ." Miss Georgina stopped when Martin frowned at her.

"Maybe it is, and maybe it ain't."

I grinned. Anytime Martin began a sentence with that phrase, something else was sure to follow. He didn't disappoint us.

"Where there's smoke there's fire, and I think we need to look for more sparks before we go runnin' to the sheriff."

"I agree." Miss Jane nodded emphatically.

Benjamin shrugged. "Okay, but you know if you withhold

evidence you could go to jail."

"Oh!" Miss Georgina's face puckered. "We'd better get this to the sheriff right away."

"Georgina, calm down. If Bob was going to arrest us, he'd have done it long ago."

Martin could have a point there. Like the time we broke into Corky's apartment when we thought he was involved in Miss Aggie's disappearance. Or the time we entered a crime scene with yellow tape warning us off.

"Maybe I'd be safer in jail." Miss Aggie's voice trembled and had risen to a shrill tone. "Maybe I'll just call Bob and tell him to lock me up for a while."

"Oh, but surely you can't think you're in danger." Miss Aggie wasn't normally timid, but this wasn't the first time she'd almost gone to pieces when a death occurred.

"I *am* a *Pennington*, you know. Who's to say I'm *not* in danger?"

The phone rang, and I excused myself.

"Cedar Lodge."

"Miss Storm?" The female voice was unfamiliar.

"Yes, this is Victoria Storm."

"My name is Laura Baker. I'm Clyde Foster's daughter, calling from St. Louis. I understand you're the person who discovered my father's body." She paused, and I heard her breathing heavily.

"Yes, I did. I'm so sorry for your loss, Ms. Baker." A daughter? This was news to me.

"Yes, well." She hesitated and then continued. "Would you be willing to meet with me while I'm in Cedar Chapel?"

"Yes, of course. But I've told Sheriff Turner all I know."

"I'm sure you have, but perhaps you'll think of something more if we talk for a while." Once more the hesitation. "To be honest, Miss Storm, I'm not entirely certain my father's death was an accident."

CHAPTER ▐▐ ▐▐▐ THREE

I stepped inside the pet store and paused, half expecting to hear Whatzit's cheery greeting.

"Miss Storm?" The woman who walked toward me appeared to be late middle-aged, with graying hair and sad eyes.

"Yes, I'm Victoria Storm." I took the hand she extended.

The German shepherd puppies across the room started a racket, and Laura Baker smiled and shook her head.

"Won't you come upstairs? I'm not in the mood to try to talk above the din. Anyway, my daughter is preparing tea for us."

We went upstairs, and she motioned me to a matching pair of chairs in the corner. Chairs that hadn't been there when I searched the place. Apparently Mrs. Baker planned to be comfortable while she was here. I was relieved to see the window open, allowing fresh air into the room.

A young woman, carrying a tray with tea things, came through the door from the tiny kitchen. She stared at me through dark brown eyes that turned up slightly at the outer corners. I suspected the effect was from cosmetics. She set the tray on the table between her mother and me, then pulled up the desk chair. She sat and crossed her legs.

"Miss Storm, this is my daughter, Christiana."

I held out my hand toward the girl, and she stared at it silently for a few seconds before giving it a brief shake. Her sullen look detracted from a face that should have been beautiful. Black hair fell in waves halfway down her back, and the pouty lips looked like something out of the magazines that women didn't want their husbands looking at.

I wasn't sure why, but something about her made me extremely uncomfortable.

Laura poured tea then settled back against the cushion and cleared her throat.

"I appreciate your coming here today. I'm sure you're busy. I understand you own and operate a boardinghouse for senior citizens."

"Yes. But I don't mind. Although as I told you on the phone, I'm not sure what I can tell you that you don't already know."

I related the incident of finding Clyde and calling the sheriff. I told her exactly what I saw when Buster and I entered the room.

"I don't know if the sheriff told you or not, but we have the parrot at Cedar Lodge. One of the ladies there is taking care of him."

"The parrot? Do you mean Whatzit is still alive?" For the first time, animation appeared on Christiana's countenance.

"Alive and well."

"I'd forgotten about Whatzit." Laura chuckled. "My mother hated that parrot."

"But why did you take him home with you?" Christiana demanded. Hostility blazed from her eyes. "Who gave you that right?"

"Tiana! Don't be rude." Laura frowned at her daughter, then gave me an apologetic look.

"Miss Aggie was a good friend of Clyde's. She often took care of Whatzit when he had to be out of town overnight." I spoke directly to Laura, deliberately avoiding the accusing eyes of her daughter. "The poor bird was very distraught, screeching uncontrollably. Apparently he was with Clyde when he died."

"I'm sure it was very kind of the lady to take care of my father's parrot. Please excuse my daughter. She never had a chance to meet her grandfather, and his death has upset her."

"Of course, I understand." Although to me, the girl appeared more angry than grieved, but then I didn't know her.

"Mrs. Baker, you said you questioned if your father's death was an accident." I wasn't about to let that one go unexplored. "Would you mind explaining what you meant?"

"It's more a feeling than anything else." She bit her lip and turned clouded eyes to me. "You see, my mother suspected for years that he'd been involved in something illegal. She was afraid of something. Whether some sort of retribution or not, I don't know. She never said. But I think that's why she left him when she found out she was expecting a child. Me."

"But that was years ago. What would make you think it's connected to his death?"

"I'm not sure. But don't you think the circumstances are strange?"

Of course I thought they were, but I wasn't ready to tell her that. Or to reveal any of the suspicions we had concerning Clyde's death.

"Have you mentioned your concerns to Sheriff Turner?"

She sighed. "Yes, unfortunately. He patted me on the arm and told me not to let my imagination run away with me."

No surprise. I knew from experience that even if he took her seriously he wouldn't let on.

I took a last sip of tea and stood. "Laura, if there's anything I can do, please don't hesitate to call me."

"Thank you again for coming. And if you think of anything else, please let me know."

I gave her a noncommittal nod and then realized I was doing the same thing to her that Sheriff Turner always did to me. But it couldn't be helped. Not until I was sure I could trust her.

I turned to Christiana and smiled. She turned away abruptly and began to gather up the tea things.

Sweeten up your attitude, young lady. The same words my grandmother used to say to me now ran through my head toward Christiana Baker.

I grinned as I descended the stairs and let myself out of the shop. But as I started the van and headed home, I could still see the venom coming from the girl's eyes. Why in the world was she so hostile to me? Or was that just her nature? Maybe I was taking her bad manners too personally. Imagining something that wasn't there.

But I was pretty sure someone had killed Clyde. For all I knew, it could have been Laura and her daughter. Although, I had no idea what their motive would be.

I arrived at the lodge to find no one there except Mabel. She was dusting the mantel in the great room. I stood and looked at the picture of my third-great-grandfather, Franklin

Storm, who'd come to this country as an indentured servant.

Mabel started as she turned and saw me standing in the doorway.

"Mercy, I didn't hear you come in. You should have said something."

"Sorry, I was deep in thought, I guess." I grinned, and she grinned back.

"Where is everyone?"

"Every last one of them went to the senior center, and they're all staying there for lunch."

"Oh, then you don't need to bother to cook. I'll just grab a sandwich and eat at my desk."

I started to leave, then turned back. "Mabel! Why are you cleaning? You don't have to do that."

"Go on about your business," she said, shaking the feather duster my way. "It won't hurt you to take a little help, and it won't hurt me to do it. You can't take care of this big place by yourself."

"Okay, in that case, thanks. I can, without a doubt, use the help." The only housekeeping staff I had at the moment was a teenage girl who helped out on Saturdays. I'd been planning to put an ad in the paper but hadn't gotten around to it yet.

Sandwich in hand, I sat at my desk and picked up the account book. I stared at it a moment, then laid it aside and opened the drawer where I kept writing materials.

It was time to organize my thoughts, and for me, that meant starting a list.

Clyde Foster: Victim of accident or murder?

Clues:

1. Whatzit's frantic cries of "No, no, get out."
2. Fragment of paper with letters n-n-e-l.
3. Suspicion of Clyde's illegal activities.

Possible Suspects:

1. Laura Baker (But why would she question the accident theory if she'd killed him?)
2. Christiana Baker?

I read the list over. This was pathetic, I had no evidence whatsoever. Only a hunch and a big imagination. I tossed the notebook and pen into the drawer and went to work on the accounts. By the time the seniors came home at three o'clock, I'd made a pretty good dent in the paperwork.

"Victoria! Where are you?" A moment later, Miss Georgina burst into the room, followed closely by Miss Jane and Miss Aggie.

"Aggie was right, Victoria." Miss Jane's eyes sparkled with excitement. "Clyde was murdered."

"It seems that way," Miss Georgina added.

"Yes," said Miss Aggie. "And it's a good thing we searched the shop when we did, because Bob has declared it a crime scene."

☙

I wasn't surprised when Sheriff Turner called and asked me to come to his office. I ran upstairs to grab a sweater, as the temperature had started dropping again around noon.

When I got to the van, I found Miss Aggie in the front passenger seat, and the rest of the seniors occupied the second and third seats. I knew from their determined faces it wouldn't do any good to protest. They weren't about to miss whatever might happen. I was relieved to notice that Miss Aggie seemed to have conquered her fears. At least she hadn't made any immediate plans to leave.

Tom Lewis gave us a sour look as we crowded through the door.

"The sheriff only needs Victoria. The rest of you might as well go home because you're not going back there."

His voice revealed his doubt that anyone would pay attention to him.

"Would you please tell Bob we're here, Tom?" Miss Evalina gave the deputy a pointed look.

"Okay, fine." He threw his arms up and headed back to Sheriff Turner's office.

The front door opened, and Benjamin walked in.

"Mabel told me what's going on. Thought I'd join you."

Martin cackled. "Yeah, like he's gonna let a reporter in there."

"Ben, you shouldn't have come!" Miss Aggie snapped. "Now they probably won't let anyone in but Victoria."

Which proved to be true, and which was fine with me.

All I had to do was repeat what I'd told the sheriff before, sign a statement, and then I was out of there.

As the seniors headed for the van, Benjamin took my arm and stopped me. "Don't forget our date tonight."

Actually, I had forgotten that Benjamin and I had plans to have dinner at the Japanese restaurant in Caffee Springs.

"Of course I won't forget. I've been looking forward to it." Or I would have been if I'd remembered. Just a little fib to spare his feelings.

og

Miss Evalina and Frank went to their room to rest before dinner, but all the others headed for the rec room to watch TV.

I decided to relax in a warm bubble bath and almost fell
asleep in the tub. I dried off, got dressed, and was downstairs
when Benjamin arrived in his truck.

It was a beautiful, clear night, the star-decked autumn
sky like a soft curtain hanging above us, hiding us from
the world as we rode down the blacktop highway to Caffee
Springs. I leaned back against the soft leather and drank in
the enjoyment of being alone with Benjamin.

The restaurant was full, and we waited nearly thirty
minutes for a private table, even though we had reservations.

Seated at last at a small table in a corner, I breathed in
a long breath of satisfaction and smiled across at Ben. He
grinned, reached over, and took my hand, stroking my engagement ring.

Dinner was delicious, and as we talked, I could feel myself
unwinding. I knew I needed to talk to Benjamin about Laura
and her daughter but hesitated to ruin the moment.

I leaned back and watched Ben as he finished his dessert.
We'd known each other since we were children, and sometimes
I took his good looks and wonderful personality for granted.
But not tonight. I gazed at his deep blue eyes and the sandy
lock of hair that fell over his forehead.

He looked up and grinned, and then his face softened. "If
I didn't know better, I'd think the lady was in love with me,"
he teased.

"You'd think right, sir."

"Okay. I can see it in your eyes, right through that look of love. What's on your mind? Besides me?"

"I'm sorry, Ben. I don't want to spoil our evening, but there is something that concerns me."

"Something about Clyde's death, right?"

"I'm not sure." And I wasn't. "I met Clyde's daughter today. And his granddaughter."

"Oh, you met Laura and Christiana? Nice, aren't they?"

I felt my mouth fall open and shut it firmly. I should have known Benjamin would have met them. After all, he did own the newspaper and lived and breathed reporting. He probably met them before I did.

"Nice? Laura seems nice. I'd hardly use that word to describe Christiana."

"Why not? She was very nice to me."

Yeah, I'll just bet she was. So that was her game.

I shot him a glare. "Christiana's 'niceness' isn't what I wanted to talk to you about. Laura suspected her father was murdered even before the sheriff declared the shop a crime scene."

"You're kidding. She didn't hint at that to me."

"Oh, really? I wonder why not, Benjamin."

"Yeah, she probably thought I'd write it up in the *Gazette*." He frowned. "Still. . ."

"It seems Laura's mother had told her about some shady dealings Clyde was involved in. That's why she left him. She was afraid." I paused, gauging his reaction. "That's why Laura has this feeling about her dad being murdered."

"Hmm, it looks like she could be right. I doubt Turner would have declared it a crime scene without evidence."

"I wonder if he'll let them stay in Clyde's apartment until after the funeral." There were a lot of cabins for rent in the vicinity, but the closest decent hotel was at least ten miles away.

"I don't know, but they're not leaving right after the funeral."

"They're not? Why not?"

"I don't know. But Christiana applied for the job at the *Gazette*."

I shut my eyes and drew a deep breath. "The secretarial position, you mean?"

"Yeah. You know we've needed someone for a while."

I waited.

The look he threw my way was definitely worried, if not downright guilty.

"You hired her," I stated.

"Why not? She's qualified." He shrugged. "Oh, come on, Victoria. Don't be jealous just because she's pretty."

"What? I'll have you know I'm not jealous. I just don't like her. She was very hostile toward me." And he thought she was pretty.

"I'm sure it's just your imagination, Vickie."

"Excuse me. I know what I saw. And don't call me Vickie." How dare he call me jealous, and how dare he call me Vickie. He knew I hated it. That is, I used to hate it. Not so much this last year or two, but I hated it now.

"Come on, honey. I don't know what the problem is here. If it bothers you that much, I'll tell her I've changed my mind." He reached across the table and took my hand.

I sighed. Was I just jealous? God had dealt with me about

that last year, and I thought I'd overcome it. But the thought of Benjamin spending time with that little vixen made me cringe. Still. . .I needed to grow up. And I trusted Ben.

"No, I'm sorry. I overreacted. I'm sure you're right. I must have imagined her attitude to be worse than it was." There. "I'm all right with it, Ben."

"Sure?"

"Yes, sure." In a pig's eye. Oops. *Sorry, Lord.*

We talked about other things on the ride back to Cedar Chapel. After all, the little squabble was over. Only I didn't feel like it was over. We kissed good night at my door, and I went inside.

I went to my office, took the notebook and pen out of the drawer, and scratched out the question mark by Christiana's name. I then added three exclamation points, tossed the pen on the desk, and went up to bed.

CHAPTER FOUR

After breakfast the next morning, Miss Aggie asked me to watch out for Whatzit while she went to Pennington House to help. They were doing last-minute decorating at this point, and she couldn't bear to stay away. The rest of the seniors stated their intentions of going to the senior center. I grabbed Miss Jane and Miss Georgina before they could take off.

"Could I talk to you two for a few minutes?"

The nervous glances they darted at one another caused a pang of guilt to run through me. I should probably stop using these two sweet ladies as my information highway.

"Why don't we go in the parlor? It's more comfy."

I linked arms with them and escorted them in.

"Now Victoria, I don't know what you're up to, but we have to hurry. There's bingo at the center this morning, and we don't want to be late."

"You won't be. I promise." I smiled and sat on the wing chair beside the fireplace.

With obvious reluctance, Miss Jane and Miss Georgina sat on one of the sofas.

"Okay, all I want to know is if either of you knew that

Clyde had a wife and daughter."

"We knew he had a wife, of course. But that was years ago," Miss Jane said. "He met her in New York, married her, and brought her home with him."

New York? That's where Aggie's brother, Forrest, lived and worked after college. His mother's family owned a textile business there.

"Was Clyde there visiting Forrest?"

Miss Jane shrugged. "He never told me why he was there. And I wasn't about to ask him."

"Me either." Miss Georgina shivered. "I stayed as far away from Clyde as I could."

They'd told me before that Clyde had a cruel streak when they were young. Miss Aggie was the only one of the girls in their group he hadn't terrorized, and that was because she was his hero's little sister.

"So, tell me about Clyde's wife."

"I didn't know her except to say hello in passing. You didn't either, did you, Georgina?"

"No, but I always felt sorry for her. I wasn't much surprised when she left him."

"What about their daughter?"

Miss Jane shrugged. "His wife left him a few months after they married. Maybe she was expecting when she left."

I nodded and told them about my meeting with Laura and Christiana the day before.

"You don't say." Miss Jane's eyes were wide. "A granddaughter, too."

"Clyde never mentioned it, that I know of." Miss

Georgina's silver curls bounced when she shook her head.

"He probably didn't know." Miss Jane's eyes glinted. "If I'd been in his wife's place, I sure wouldn't have told him. In fact, I don't know how he ever got anyone to marry him in the first place."

It was obvious the two friends had exhausted their supply of information on the subject, so I stood. "Thank you so much. And I hope you both win at bingo."

Georgina giggled. "We're playing for a pie from Samson's Bakery. Maybe we can furnish tonight's dessert."

I hoped not. I'd much rather have Mabel's freshly made cobbler than the day-old pastries Mr. Samson donated to the senior center.

I stepped into the kitchen and was met by a beaming Mabel.

"Bobby will bring Sarah next weekend. He's going to stay until Monday to get her enrolled in school. Thank you so much, Victoria, for making a way for me to keep my job here."

"We couldn't do without you, Mabel. And I'm sure it'll be nice to have a child around." I wasn't exactly sure, but I was sure praying the little girl wouldn't be anything like the Hansen kids across the street. Even Buster shied away from them since they'd thrown over-ripe tomatoes from their father's garden at him.

I went to my suite on the third floor. I'd remodeled Grandfather's library and Grandmother's sitting room last year, and for the first few months, every time I walked through the door I seemed to sense their presence. But gradually the rooms had become my own. A haven for rest and to gather my thoughts together.

I got cleaning supplies from the small utility closet at the end of the hall and polished all the furniture in both rooms, then cleaned my bathroom. The carpet had been freshly vacuumed the day before. The outside windows could use a cleaning, but they'd have to wait until a warmer day. Maybe I'd call someone and have them done. Finances were getting better, and the two remodeled bedrooms on this floor were ready for occupancy. I'd had to turn down boarders several times in the last few months. There were several on the waiting list, so I decided to make some calls and let them know I had rooms available. The first two I called were no longer interested, but the third almost screeched in my ear with excitement. She promised to call back and let me know when she could come look at the room.

The fourth was an elderly man who was tired of living with his daughter.

"I love those grandkids, but sometimes they drive me crazy." A bellowing laugh followed to show he was joking. He said he'd be in Cedar Chapel the following week to meet me and view the room.

Seating myself in Grandma's rocker by the front window, I browsed through the mail I'd ignored the day before.

A letter from my mother lay on top where I'd deposited it. I ripped it open, and a photo fell out. Mom and Dad in beach clothes with wide-brimmed hats atop their heads. Mom was grinning, and Dad looked pained. As though he'd rather be somewhere else. Which I had no doubt he did.

I pulled out the single sheet of paper and read the two paragraphs. Nothing new. Same old, same old.

Mom loved the Bahamas and planned to stay for a while, but Dad was leaving for Rome on a business trip. Familiar loneliness clutched at my stomach, and I swiped a hand across my eyes. I would not cry. After all these years you'd think I wouldn't care anymore. And I'd had Grandma and Grandpa. And the lodge. I'd always loved the lodge. Once a real lodge, it had been the Storm family's private home for many years. I'd spent all my summers and most holidays here when I was growing up. The rest of the time I was away at boarding school, while Dad did business around the world and Mom did whatever she did in her social whirl of a life. After Grandpa died, Grandma had turned her home into a boardinghouse for seniors—mostly lifelong friends. But it came as a complete surprise when Grandma had left Cedar Lodge to me in her will.

I went through the rest of my mail then went down to take care of the seniors' rooms. Most of them were already spotless, but I checked for bed linens that might need to be changed early.

I laughed silently when I entered Martin's room. Comics were stacked up in three piles. His collection. Those, I wouldn't dare touch.

When I went into Miss Aggie's room, Whatzit glared at me as though he'd like to peck out my eyes. He liked me about as well as Clyde had.

When I finally made it down to the first floor, wonderful smells drew me to the kitchen.

"What's for lunch, Mabel? It smells delish."

"Mexican meat loaf. I found the recipe online the other day. Sounded like something you'd like, so I thought I'd make it for lunch when the seniors weren't here."

Everyone knew I loved Mexican food. Most of the seniors liked it too, but I'd pretty much burned them out on it when I was doing some of the cooking before Mabel came.

The meat loaf was as good as it smelled, and I asked Mabel to keep the recipe on file.

After lunch I went to my office and pulled out the list again.

Beside Laura's name, I put a notation. *Seeking revenge for her mother?*

I frowned at Christiana's name and wondered if she'd started working for Ben yet. I reached for the phone and began to punch-in his office number, then slammed the phone down. How pathetic was I? Besides, if she answered she'd probably figure out why I called. I wasn't about to give her the satisfaction.

Maybe I'd call his cell instead, just to hear his voice and ask him if his new secretary was working out. As I reached for the phone again, the front door opened.

"Victoria?" Phoebe's voice rang out. "Where are you?"

CB

Phoebe Collins and I were complete opposites. While I was insecure and sometimes shy around strangers, she liked everyone and figured they liked her, too. Bouncy and outgoing, she drew me out of myself and taught me how to have fun again. I'd known her as the bank teller where I made my deposits, and that was about it, until Corky fell head-over-heels in love with the blue-eyed, blond beauty. Since then, she and I had become best friends. The first real friend, except for Ben and the seniors, I'd had since leaving

Dallas to take over the lodge.

"Phoebe. Aren't you working today?"

"Yes." She laughed. "But I had to tell you something. Face-to-face. Uncle Jack's coming this weekend."

My stomach jumped. Why did Jack Riley show up every time someone got murdered around here? Raised in Cedar Chapel, he'd left at a young age to eventually own an import/export business in Germany. Until last year, when he'd arrived for an unexpected visit, Phoebe had never met the uncle she'd heard about and admired all her life. While here, he had regaled them with tales of his exploits during World War II and afterwards. At the time I'd suspected him of being guilty of selling jewels stolen from the Jewish victims before and during the Holocaust years. But when Mr. Riley had helped solve the murder at Pennington House, I'd decided I might have misjudged him.

But here he was, popping up again after a suspicious death had occurred.

"Really? That's great, Phoebe. Why is he coming to the states?"

"Well, silly. Because he wants to see us, of course."

"Of course. I am silly."

"I have to run. I'm almost late back to work."

Okay, but I wanted to know more about Jack Riley's sudden visit. "Why don't you and Corky come to dinner tonight?"

"Wonderful idea. Will you call Corky and ask if it's okay with him?"

"Sure thing. See you later."

She rushed away, and I went to the office and punched in

the number to Corky's cell. He answered on the second ring.

"Hey, Victoria." Huh? Oh. You'd think by now I'd be used to caller ID.

"Hi, Corky. How goes everything out there?"

"Great. Aunt Aggie's ordering around all the interior decorators as though they were small children instead of professionals with degrees." He laughed.

"I just invited Phoebe to dinner tonight. Are you free?"

"Are you kidding? If my girl's going to be there? I'll call the bank and tell her I'll pick her up."

"Good. See you later."

The seniors arrived home around two o'clock, and they all went upstairs to take naps. They started to trail back downstairs a couple of hours later, most of them settling into the recreation room in front of the big-screen TV.

I peeked in, thinking I might join them, but when I saw the black-and-white cowboy movie jumping across the screen, I hurriedly turned away. Of course, it could be worse. Martin's favorite old-time actor was W. C. Fields.

I made a quick call to Ben and invited him to dinner. He and Corky had become fast friends over the last couple of years, which made it nice for Phoebe and me.

"I'll be there," Ben said.

Before I knew it, the words tumbled out of my mouth. "Has Christiana started working yet?"

"Yes, is that still bothering you?" I distinctly heard a sigh. "I told you I wouldn't hire her if it bothered you."

"Don't jump to conclusions. It doesn't *bother* me. I just wondered if she'd started yet."

"Okay, that's good. She's doing a really good job, and I'd

hate to have to let her go."

Yeah, I'll just bet he would. Oops. I was doing it again. "I'll see you later then. Bye." I needed to control my emotions better.

"Bye, sweetheart."

I sighed. I probably didn't deserve a sweet guy like Benjamin, even if he had been my tormentor when we were kids. Actually, he'd mostly been my dog Sparky's tormentor. However, Ben had turned out very well, in spite of my expectations to the contrary.

Corky and Phoebe arrived at six fifteen, and Benjamin's Avalanche pulled up a few minutes later.

"Benjamin and Corky. What fun." Miss Aggie chortled. She adored her nephew, and I knew Ben came in a close second. She tolerated Phoebe and me.

We sat down to dinner at seven. Mabel had prepared everything buffet style before she went home. She'd fried chicken, much to Ben's delight. I hoped for his sake she would never leave us, because my fried chicken always turned out greasy and undercooked.

"How's the hotel coming along?" Frank asked. Miss Aggie had forbidden anyone to come to Pennington House for the last few weeks, wanting to surprise us on opening day.

"Just a few finishing touches and we're ready to go." Corky's voice held excitement. His dream had been to restore Pennington House to its original splendor and convert it to a posh restaurant/hotel. From the joy in his eyes, I was pretty sure he wasn't disappointed.

"Okay, Phoebe," I said. "I know you're bursting to tell everyone your news, so go ahead."

She laughed, her eyes lighting up. "Uncle Jack is coming this weekend."

A murmur of pleasure rose from the seniors. Miss Georgina clapped her hands. "Oh, good. He can tell us more stories."

"Maybe he's sick and tired of always having to tell us stories, Georgina," Martin piped up. "Ever think of that?"

Miss Georgina's face crumpled. "Oh, I didn't think about that." Clearly distressed, she appeared to be near tears.

"Aw, I was just kidding." Martin reached over and patted her hand. A few months ago, we'd all have been shocked, but we'd come to realize a budding romance between those two. I hoped Martin would learn to think before he spoke instead of always having to comfort her after the fact.

Miss Jane glared at him but didn't say anything.

"I wonder why he's coming at this time." I leaned back, eager to see what response that would get.

"Why, I told you, Victoria. He misses Mom and me."

"Hmm." Frank was staring at me. "It does seem sort of odd, with Clyde's murder and all. Seems every time he comes, someone just got killed."

Phoebe gasped, and Frank looked ashamed. "I didn't mean anything by that, Phoebe."

"Don't start again, Victoria," Corky snapped, glaring at me. "I thought we'd settled that Phoebe's uncle isn't involved in anything illegal. Especially murder."

"Why, I didn't say—"

"Oh Victoria, you don't suspect Uncle Jack of being involved in Clyde's murder, do you?" Phoebe stared at me.

"Of course not. Why does everyone always think I'm

accusing him? I'm not. All I asked was a simple question. Frank's the one who mentioned the murder."

"Yeah. But I didn't mean it. Like I said, I got carried away. Sorry, Phoebe." Frank leaned closer to Miss Evalina, who patted his hand.

I glanced at Ben. He sat looking at me with a lopsided smile.

"What?"

"What, indeed?"

He knew me too well.

CHAPTER FIVE

Why did I have such a sensitive conscience? After battling with it for the past half hour, I had to face facts. Withholding evidence was against the law, and the Bible said to obey the law. So, didn't that mean I was committing sin by not turning the fragment Miss Aggie'd found in the bedpost over to Bob Turner?

With one finger, I slid open the bottom drawer—the one I'd unlocked and stared at for the last thirty minutes. The fragment lay on top of a box of checkbooks. The faded letters on the paper seemed to jump out at me.

Oh, all right. I took the fragment out, then relocked the drawer. The seniors would be furious with me for going without them, but I wasn't about to have them involved if the sheriff decided to drag me over the coals for keeping it from him. Besides, they'd just be sitting down to lunch at the center about now, and I didn't want to wait.

I should probably change, but why bother? It was just the sheriff. I grabbed a jacket from the hall closet, slipping it on as I went into the kitchen. Mabel was whistling "Amazing Grace" as she stirred something in a cast-iron skillet.

Curious, I stepped closer. I caught my breath. She was

caramelizing sugar. Was she. . . ? "Mabel, are you making caramel pie?"

"Yep." She grinned. "Miss Eva told me your grandma used to make 'em for you all the time."

My eyes flooded, and I blinked back tears. Grandma had hated making caramel pie, but she did it all the same, at least once a month, each time I was at Cedar Chapel. Just to please me.

"That's right. She did. It was my favorite dessert. I haven't tasted one since Grandma died. Thank you, Mabel."

"Ain't nothing." Apparently just noticing my coat, she nodded. "Going out, eh?"

"Yes, I have a little business to take care of. I shouldn't be long. Do you need anything while I'm out?"

"No, shopping's all done."

I waved and went through the door that connected to the garage. I hopped into the van, wondering if it was time to get myself a smaller car for when I traveled alone. I'd been trying to talk myself into it for months. Just like I'd tried to convince myself I needed a cell phone. Actually it was Ben who insisted I get a cell phone for emergencies. But I hated to take on more monthly payments until finances improved.

I passed High Street, drove another block, and turned at the square. Ah. A parking spot right in front of the court-house. I got out, locked the door, and hurried inside to the sheriff's office.

Tom Lewis looked up as I walked in, and a pained expression crossed his face. I ignored the groan that rumbled from his throat.

"Good morning, Tom." I might as well be pleasant. It

couldn't hurt anything. "I'd like to see Sheriff Turner if he's available."

Was that suspicion on Tom's face? And after I'd been so nice?

"He's busy."

Okay, I would not act annoyed. "Will you please see if he can talk to me for a minute? It's important."

He snorted. "Yeah, I'll bet it is."

Okay, enough was enough. I leaned over the counter and glared into his eyes. "Listen, you twerp, I'm going to see Bob Turner. Do you want to announce me, or do I barge in?" Uh-oh. Had I really said that? I whispered a silent apology upward.

"Victoria. Get in here." Bob Turner stood in his office doorway, glaring.

Oops. Not a good way to get things started.

I walked past the sheriff, hoping I didn't look as nervous as I felt. "Hi, Sheriff Turner."

"Sit down." He sat behind his desk and motioned to the chair in front of it. He steepled his fingers and stared at me.

"I want you to stop coming in here and trying to intimidate my deputy."

"But he—"

"Uh-uh." He shook his finger. "Don't want to hear it."

"Fine." I folded my arms and leaned back.

"Now, what do you want?" He picked up a pencil and tapped it on his desk.

Maybe I shouldn't have come. Maybe this was a big mistake.

I took a deep breath then plunged in. "I found something in Clyde's apartment."

His hand slammed down on the desk, and then he jumped up. "Are you telling me you broke into a crime scene?"

My chair vibrated from the volume of his voice. Or maybe it was my shaking that caused it.

"No!" I yelled back. Two could play his screaming game.

He sat, leaned back, and I wondered if he were counting to ten.

"Listen," I said as calmly as I could manage, "I looked around the place when we went back to get Whatzit's big cage. You'd already been over the place and hadn't said anything about it being a crime scene at the time."

He inhaled and exhaled slowly. "Okay. What did you find and where?"

I reached into my coat pocket and pulled out the fragment of paper. With a great deal of reluctance, I handed it over. But at least I was doing the right thing. I hoped.

Sheriff glanced at the scrap and scratched his head. He looked at me as though I'd just sprouted horns.

"What is this?"

"Look, Sheriff." I hopped up and went around to his side. Bending over, I pointed to the letters *n-n-e-l*.

He frowned and turned the paper sideways, then back. "So?"

"Tunnel. It has to mean tunnel. Like the ones at Pennington House."

He snorted. "Or maybe funnel, or kennel, or any number of words. For crying out loud, Victoria. Why do you have to imagine things?"

Indignant, I went back to my chair and sat. "Fine. Scoff if you like. But who would hide a note about a kennel or a funnel in a bedpost?"

"Bedpost? You broke his bedpost?" He jumped up again then ran his hands through his hair.

I felt a giggle coming on. "Of course not. The knob was loose. Miss. . .I mean. . .I saw it was loose, so I unscrewed it. And voila, there was this mysterious scrap of paper."

"Umm-hmm. I don't think it's anything, but thanks for bringing it to me."

I leaned forward. "You mean you're not going to check it out?"

"Victoria, will you leave the police work to me? Go home and take care of your old folks."

I sat and stewed for a few seconds, wondering if I should push him any further. "Oh, by the way, Miss Aggie figured out what Whatzit has been trying to say."

"Just sounded like squawking to me. I figgered he was upset about Clyde not bringing his dinner." He chuckled.

"You figured wrong. He's screaming, 'No, no, get out!' "

At a choking sound from behind me, I looked over my shoulder to see Tom slapping his knee and laughing. Turning back, I caught a smirk on the sheriff's face, which he tried to hide.

"Fine. Laugh all you want." I jumped up. "But you know that bird talks. And Miss Aggie's been around him long enough to interpret his squawks."

Standing as tall as possible, I lifted my head and stalked from the room. I guess the effect was ruined when I tripped over a loose tile. A burst of laughter sounded from the office. I considered faking a fall and suing them but quickly repented.

My mood changed as I stepped out into the fresh air. At least I didn't get tossed into jail. I was free. I tilted back my head and inhaled the chilly air. A wonderful aroma sent another thought running through my mind. I'd left home without eating lunch, and Hannah's was only a block away. Probably packed full at this time, but I needed a crowd right now. I should have changed clothes after all. Oh well, they'd seen me in faded jeans before.

I went in and glanced around the crowded café. The elderly Borden twins, Fred and Ted, were getting up from a booth halfway down from where I stood. I headed there quickly, and when they'd left, I plopped myself down on the red vinyl, expecting to have to wait. But Hannah was at my side in a flash.

"I'll get this table cleaned off for you, sweetie, and then I'll bring your water and a menu."

I smiled as she placed the dishes on a tray, wiped the table with a damp cloth, then swiped a dry towel over it. "Got stiffed, didn't you?"

"Oh hon, I'd bet my grandma's silver that those two haven't tipped anyone in their whole life."

She took off with the tray and was back in less than a minute with my menu and water. Now why was she giving me the VIP treatment when she had customers stretching their necks to see why she wasn't waiting on them?

Before I had a chance to open the menu, she took out her ticket book, turned over to a new page, and said, "Now, what's this I hear about Clyde Foster's death being a murder?"

Groaning, I thought fast. I wasn't about to get into this discussion with Hannah, especially with half the town within earshot.

CB

"So you told her everything?"

I wouldn't have minded the dismay in Benjamin's voice, but the amusement teed me off. He'd stopped by shortly after I got home from lunch, and we were sitting on the porch swing. I rested against the slatted back and shivered as cold ran through my body. Why was it so chilly this early in the season? And why in the world were we sitting out here in the cold when a fire was leaping and dancing and warming the parlor? "No. I did not tell her everything."

I gnawed my bottom lip. "At least not completely everything." His raised eyebrows infuriated me. "Oh, go home."

"I will not." He grinned. "Honey, don't kick yourself too much. Hannah could get top secrets out of the FBI if she put her mind to it."

"But Ben, what if the murderer was in there? Now he knows we have clues."

He put his arm around my shoulders and pulled me close. "Hmm," I sighed.

He leaned closer, and I got ready to be kissed or nibbled on the ear. "Which of our neighbors do you suspect?" he whispered.

I sat up and gave him a shove. "I'm going inside."

He laughed. "No, don't go. I'll be good. I promise."

Maybe it was time to change the subject. "How is your new secretary working out?"

"Tiana's doing great. She caught on really fast."

"Tiana?" I raised my eyebrows.

"She asked me to call her that. It's her nickname."

"Yes, I know. So, she's doing great, eh?"

"Absolutely. She's wonderful with the business people. Advertisements are picking up."

I tightened my jaw to keep from snarling. "Yeah, I'll bet."

"What do you mean by that?"

"Nothing, nothing." Maybe this choice of subject wasn't so good either. My jealousy was building steam big-time.

He turned and, putting his finger beneath my chin, lifted my face. I closed my eyes.

"Look at me, Victoria."

I shook my head. No way was I going to let him see what was in my eyes.

"Vickie. Look at me."

I opened one eye. Then the other. "What?"

"Are you jealous of Tiana?"

"Of course not, and stop calling her that."

"Why?" A bewildered look crinkled his face.

Duh. Because it sounds like a term of endearment? Like when you call me Vickie? "Oh, I don't know. I have to go inside now. I need to mop the kitchen floor."

"All right, sweetheart, but you don't need to worry. Tiana is my secretary. Nothing more."

If he didn't stop calling her that, I was going to clobber him.

We stood up, and I turned and lifted my lips for his goodbye kiss.

"See you later, honey." His kiss was light, and as he headed back to his truck, I already missed him. He opened the door then turned around. "Oh, I forgot. I have a meeting tonight. I'll stop by tomorrow."

I went inside feeling rejected and unloved. *Stop that,*

Victoria. You're behaving like a fourteen-year-old girl. No, twelve.

The house was empty except for Mabel finishing up the dinner preparations. She left at two on Friday but always made a roast or meat loaf—something easy to warm up—and there would be a salad in the refrigerator. Even the smell of caramel pie didn't lift my spirits. What if Ben were falling for that seductive young woman? What if I lost him?

Mabel left. I dusted the furniture in both parlors, then went to the great hall. I lifted my eyes to Franklin Storm's portrait—the man who'd founded this town. He'd bought up miles and miles of land, finally dividing the acres into separate lots and selling a large portion to his friends. The town of Cedar Chapel was part of his original landholdings. He'd built this room. The first Cedar Lodge. A real lodge in those days. His descendants had added room after room, and then the second and third floors.

Usually I found comfort in this room. But not today. Somehow the pride I'd always harbored concerning my heritage felt like a character flaw. Like jealousy. I'd always thought I was a pretty good person. A true Christian. Maybe I'd been kidding myself. I was full of sin. I was a proud, jealous lawbreaker. Yes, there was no denying it. I broke laws. Like going into places I shouldn't and searching people's private belongings. Clyde's wasn't the first. But the jealousy was the worst. It was tearing me apart.

The sound of cars pulling into the garage jerked me out of my self-examination.

Laughter and squabbling rang throughout the house as the seniors filed in. Relief washed over me. My friends. They loved me.

I rushed out into the foyer. "Miss Jane, how was lunch today? Miss Georgina, did you play bingo?" My voice sounded high and overly excited even to me.

"What's wrong with you, Victoria?" Miss Jane's forehead furrowed. "The food at the center is terrible. You know we don't go there for the food."

"You know we don't play bingo on Fridays, too," Miss Georgina piped up. "Are you ill, dear? Let me see if you have a fever." She placed her plump hand on my forehead then smiled. "Cool as a cucumber."

Miss Evalina and Frank came in and went upstairs to rest.

"Anyone want to watch a movie with me?" Martin's voice didn't sound too hopeful. When Frank got married, Martin had lost his movie buddy.

Miss Jane harrumphed and headed up to her room.

"I'll watch a movie with you, Martin," Miss Georgina said, her eyes fluttering.

Martin's eyes lit up; then he cleared his throat. "Okay, but we're not watching no girl movie."

"All right, Martin." She trailed after him on her tiny feet.

I put Buster in the basement, got the mop and bucket from the broom closet, and set about scrubbing the kitchen and storage room.

After that was done, I went downstairs to the basement. I'd finish up the laundry while the floors dried. Buster threw me an accusing look for banishing him to the nether regions.

"Don't look at me like that. It's your own fault." He probably had forgotten all about the time he'd tracked mud onto my freshly scrubbed floor, but I sure hadn't.

I took a load of towels from the washer and tossed them

into the dryer, then loaded sheets in the washer and turned it on.

"C'mon, boy. Let's go for a walk." I grabbed his extra leash from beside the basement door. No sense staying down here while we waited.

Buster's ears popped to attention, and he scrambled up, wagging his tail and nudging my hand. I laughed and scratched him behind one ear.

We walked up the steps to the side yard and headed for the front of the house. Buster strained against his leash, wanting to run. We started down the sidewalk at a jog.

"Victoria, yoo-hoo!"

Oh no. Why didn't I have enough sense to go the other way?

Mrs. Miller, my next-door neighbor, came stumbling across her lawn in high heels. Good grief.

I put on a smile and waved. After all, she'd been one of Grandma's friends, although I'd been told Grandma put the woman in her place on a number of occasions. It wasn't that Janis Miller was wicked or treated people badly. But she was voracious in her quest to squeeze every last drop of gossip out of anyone she came in contact with. Especially me. She'd been wringing family secrets from me all my life.

I didn't know what she was after today, but my lips were sealed.

She tripped the last few steps to me and stood huffing and puffing until she could catch her breath. In her hand she held a yellowed, rolled-up newspaper.

"Are you all right, Mrs. Miller?" I had a terrible fear that she'd drop at my feet in a faint one day.

"Fine, just fine," she gasped.

Finally, her breathing slowed. "Whew. Taking your doggie for a walk, I see."

"Yep. He thinks he's taking me."

She laughed. "I hear you're the one who found Clyde Foster."

Okay, here it came. "Yes, ma'am."

"There's talk going around that he was murdered."

"Really?" Did my voice sound innocent or evasive?

She narrowed her eyes and planted her hands on her hips. "Don't be coy with me, Victoria."

Coy? "Sorry, I didn't mean to be."

She looked me straight in the eye, searching. I tried to keep my gaze neutral.

"Ha. That's what I thought. And it doesn't surprise me one bit that someone killed the old codger." She held the newspaper out to me. "He had it coming, the horse thief."

CHAPTER ⚏ SIX

When I'd invited Phoebe to lunch with me at Hannah's, I hadn't intended to use her as a sounding board, but I suspected that's what I'd been doing. "It seems obvious to me Clyde's death is linked to the Penningtons. Just like the last two crimes in Cedar Chapel. And all coming so closely together would indicate they're linked." Hmm. Maybe not all of them. I stared at my coffee and stirred. "That is, except for Miss Aggie's kidnapping, but even that took place at Pennington House, so maybe it was connected as well."

"I don't know." Phoebe paused and took a sip of her soda then set it back on the table. "I think you should let the sheriff handle this."

Et tu, Brute? I scrunched up my nose. "C'mon, Phoebe, I need some support here."

She giggled. "You have plenty of that. The seniors are always willing and ready to dive into a mystery."

"You've got that right." I shook my head. "I used to worry, but then I realized every time they started sleuthing they seemed more chipper than ever. I think the excitement keeps them young."

"And I agree." She set her glass down and threw her

wadded paper napkin on her empty plate. "I have to get back to work. See you at dinner. Oh, and thanks for inviting Uncle Jack. He's looking forward to seeing you all again."

"Yeah, see you later." I watched as she stopped at the register and handed her ticket and money to Betty, Hannah's new waitress. She turned and waved before she opened the door and went out.

I took the last bite of my chicken fajitas and dabbed my lips with my napkin. I'd hoped to get some feedback from Phoebe. But it looked like I was on my own.

It was time to get serious about my list. I grabbed a notepad from my purse, glad to see the pen attached to the hard cardboard back.

"Need a refill?" I glanced up to see Hannah hovering over me with a coffeepot.

"Yes, thanks." I shoved my mug closer to her and waited until she filled it and walked away.

I pursed my lips and stared at the blank page. Okay, here goes.

Who had a motive to kill Clyde?
1. His daughter?
    a. To get revenge for his treatment of her mother?
2. Christiana?
    b. Motive unknown.
3. Someone who suspected Clyde knew the location of the Pennington jewels?
4. Someone who suspected Clyde knew they were involved with the theft/disappearance of the Pennington jewels?

5. *Or could it be possible that Mrs. Miller was right*
   and Clyde had stolen Burly Anderson's prize horse?
   But Mr. Anderson was eighty-five, and his sons both
   lived in Chicago. Anyway, forty years was a long
   time to hold a grudge strong enough to kill for.

Excitement burned in me as I looked over the list. Okay, maybe it was lacking any real evidence, but at least I'd put some thoughts on paper.

I tapped my pen on the table, deep in thought.

Clues:
   1. *A fragment of a note/receipt/message with the letters*
      n-n-e-l *(tunnel?).*
   2. *Whatzit's frightened screeching of "No, no, get out."*
   3. *A 1968 copy of the* Gazette *with the story of the*
      horse theft. (Which didn't mention Clyde was a suspect.)

I frowned. Not much in the way of clues. But it was a start. I crammed my notebook and pen back in my purse and paid my check, then left Hannah's and drove back to the lodge. I needed to get the house ready for my dinner guests. Thank the Lord for Mabel. At least I didn't need to worry about dinner. The day before, I'd given her the menu for the evening, and she hadn't blinked an eye when she realized she'd have to panfry chicken for ten people.

When I stepped into the kitchen, she looked up and smiled, then continued slicing vegetables for the salad.

"Can I help out with anything before I wax the dining room floor, Mabel?"

"Floors are all done." She raked cucumber slices from the cutting board into the bowl.

I shook my head. "You make me feel guilty, like I should double your salary."

She laughed. "Don't be silly. You pay me plenty. And for stuff I enjoy doing. Never thought I'd get paid for cookin' and cleaning."

"You deserve it. Guess I'll go wax the furniture then, if you're sure you don't need me in here."

I retrieved the furniture polish and cloth and did the dining room table and sideboard, then put a clean white linen tablecloth on the table. I knew Mabel would have checked the silver and napkins, so I headed for the great hall.

When I stepped through the door, I glanced, as I always did, at the portrait. Resplendent in a dark green hunting coat and snug, tan pants, the Storm patriarch stood with a tall musket in the curve of his arm, a Bible in the other hand, clutched to his chest. I knew Franklin Storm had been a godly man, even starting a church for his family and neighbors. I'd only recently discovered through family records that he'd actually become a minister in his older years.

His lips were pressed tightly together, and his face appeared rigid, but I would have sworn a twinkle lurked in those hazel eyes. Eyes that Grandma always said looked like mine. I tilted my head and examined his face. A deep cleft lay deep in his chin, just as it did in my father's. Strange how family features could be so strong they'd last through generations.

I turned away and busied myself polishing the mantel and the rest of the antique furniture scattered about the room.

Was it wrong to be proud of my heritage? Just a few days ago I'd thought so, even repented for the pride. But now, I wasn't so sure. Feeling a link with the past was different from ancestor worship.

Oh, was I ever deep thinking today. I stood in the doorway and scanned the room. Satisfied I'd missed nothing, I went out and closed the door.

Chores over, I headed for my office and took my original list from the desk drawer. Retrieving the other from my purse, I typed both lists into a Word document and saved the file.

There, that was more like it. My files were password protected, so I didn't need to worry about anyone seeing them. Not that anyone would get on my computer anyway.

Once, when Miss Aggie was missing, we'd thought she might have left a clue to her disappearance on my computer or the one at the library. That had turned out to be a false lead. Her computer activities at the library had simply been research about posh hotels and restaurants. And she hadn't touched my computer. But I'd made a new rule that day that my computer was off-limits.

I heard the roar of Miss Jane's ancient Cadillac as she pulled into the garage, followed by Frank and Miss Evalina's new car. He'd bought it when they got married but wouldn't part with his pickup truck, which stayed parked most of the time. I glanced at my watch. Three o'clock. I'd have time to take Buster for a walk before I had to get ready for dinner. Mabel had offered to stay and serve, but I'd told her she didn't need to. We'd put everything on the sideboard buffet style, and I was sure Miss Jane would help me.

I walked into the foyer to see all five of the seniors piling in. I hadn't heard Miss Aggie's Lexus. I was surprised she'd opted to go to the center with the rest. Most days she insisted on being in the big middle of whatever was going on at Pennington House.

"Victoria, is Jack Riley still coming tonight?" Miss Aggie asked. Since she'd found out his adopted granddaughter, Samantha, was her own niece, they'd become friends. They talked on the phone often, and in June, Miss Aggie had visited the family in Germany. I still wasn't convinced he was totally innocent in all the goings-on at Pennington House. Or that he hadn't dealt in stolen property during World War II. But I'd try to reserve judgment for now.

"Yes, ma'am. They'll be here at six thirty, dinner at seven."

"Oh dear. That's very late." Miss Georgina's voice trembled.

"Georgina, don't be silly," Miss Aggie retorted, hands on hips. "You know we always eat at seven when we have guests."

Martin darted a venomous look at Miss Aggie and opened his mouth, then shut it and turned to Miss Georgina. "If you want to eat at six like we usually do, I could take you to Hannah's or the steak house in Caffee Springs."

Pink washed over Miss Georgina's plump cheeks. "Thank you, Martin. That's very kind. But I wouldn't want to miss hearing more of Mr. Riley's stories."

I grinned. This would be interesting.

"Fine. I didn't wanta go anyway. Just trying to be nice." Martin's face flamed. "Don't know why you want to listen to that windbag, though. I doubt half them stories of his are true."

Miss Jane snorted and headed to her room, following Miss Evalina and Frank, who were halfway up the stairs.

Miss Georgina twisted her hankie, misery in her pale blue eyes. "I guess we could go to Hannah's if you want to, Martin."

"Naw. I don't want to." Martin stomped off to the rec room.

Taking pity on the sweet lady, who stood staring after Martin with brimming eyes, I patted her on the shoulder. "Don't worry about him, Miss Georgina. He's just a bit jealous, I think. He'll get over it."

"Jealous? But why?"

I laughed. "Because Martin is sweet on you, honey, that's why. You're a mighty pretty lady, you know."

"I am?" A blush washed over her face, and her eyes shone.

"Of course. Now why don't you go rest awhile before dinner and let him stew a bit? It'll be good for him."

Delight filled her eyes. "Thank you, Victoria, I believe I will."

I grinned as she waltzed up the stairway. Scarlett O'Hara had nothing on her.

 os

A black-and-white cat zipped across the Edisons' yard and around their shed. Buster barked with excitement and raced after it, dragging me along like flotsam. "Buster, slow down!" A pain shot from my wrist to my shoulder as the leash tightened against my hand, yanking me hard. I knew if I didn't do something, I'd end up being dragged across the ground on my rear end, so I loosened my hand and dropped the leash. When he realized he was free, he took off, the leash trailing after.

It would be useless to try to keep up with him, so I headed

back to the sidewalk and leaned against an oak tree to catch my breath.

"Yoo-hoo! Victoria!" Mrs. Miller waved from her car window, then turned into her driveway. Maybe she'd go on inside. I could hope, at any rate.

I groaned inwardly as she slammed her door and started across the street in my direction. Of course, she had imparted an interesting piece of information about the horse theft. Sort of a thin lead, but at this point anything was better than nothing.

"Hello, Mrs. Miller. How are you this afternoon?" At least she wasn't gasping for breath this time.

"Fine, fine. I'm fine." She waved her purse at me. "But I have something else for you. I knew there was another article about Mr. Anderson's prize horse."

"Oh?" I glanced around. Where in the world was Buster?

"Yes." She reached into her purse and pulled out a sheet of copy paper.

"Here. Take a look at this." Her nod could only be called triumphant. Apparently she'd realized I hadn't taken her accusations about Clyde seriously.

I took the paper, gave it a quick glance, then did a double take. CLYDE FOSTER ARRESTED FOR HORSE THEFT.

I skimmed the article. "Did he serve any time for it?"

"No, some shyster lawyer got him off. But he was guilty, all right."

I held the article out toward her, but she waved it away. "You can keep that. I have two more copies, and if I need more, I'll go back to the library."

"Thank you. But I still don't see how it could be related

to his death. Surely you don't think old Mr. Anderson could have killed Clyde."

"No, but guess who I saw at Hannah's the night before Clyde's body was found?" She pressed her lips together.

"Who?" I asked, impatient with her dramatics.

"Gabe Anderson, that's who."

Okay, that was interesting. Gabe, Mr. Anderson's youngest son, was known to have a violent temper. This deserved looking into.

From the corner of my eye I saw Buster slink around the corner. I turned and sent him a glare. Head down, he walked slowly to me and shoved his woolly head under my hand.

"All right, you reprobate, I forgive you." I rubbed his head and grabbed his leash.

"So what are you going to do about this, Victoria?" Once more, Mrs. Miller stood, hands on hips. I figured that must be her favorite pose.

"I'll look into it, I promise. Thank you for the information." I smiled and turned to go. "I really need to get home now. We have guests coming for dinner."

Her eyes gleamed. "Yes, I know. What is Jack Riley doing back here so soon?"

Now, how did she know it was Mr. Riley? Because she knew everything, that's how. With her around, we didn't need the *Gazette*.

CB

Mabel's fried chicken had been a great success. But the caramel pies were the crowning moment. I was hard-pressed not to close my eyes and sigh when I put the first bite in my mouth. Or to make *ummm* sounds. Maybe I should have saved this and served something else for dessert. Ashamed of the selfish thought, I forced myself to leave the last bite on my plate.

Phoebe and I removed the dishes and refilled coffee and tea for those who wanted more. Jack was seated between Miss Aggie and Miss Georgina. I darted a glance at them every few minutes to make sure he wasn't being rude to them. Oh, who was I kidding? Crook or not, Jack Riley was the epitome of courtesy and kindness.

Miss Aggie was oohing and aahing over a new picture of her great-niece he'd brought her. Martin, seated across from them, sent furtive glares in their direction. A giggle started somewhere in my sternum, but I managed to stop it before it reached my lips. I still wasn't used to the tentative courtship going on between Martin and Miss Georgina.

"Victoria, could we go into the parlor?" Miss Jane asked. "It'll be more comfortable in there, and Mr. Riley could share more of his adventures with us."

Martin snorted, then coughed in a poor attempt to cover it up. Georgina sent him a worried glance and shook her head.

"I have a better idea. How about the great hall?" I figured it would lend a backdrop of ambience to Mr. Riley's stories.

Murmurs of assent met my suggestion, so we were soon seated on the deep leather chairs and sofas in front of the nearly wall-sized fireplace.

"It's very kind of you to arrange this welcome dinner for me, Miss Storm." Mr. Riley flashed a smile in my direction. The kind that had probably melted the hearts of many a lady in his younger years. Even I could feel the charisma. Eighties or not, he definitely had finesse and charm. No wonder Martin was jealous.

"Mr. Riley, how is Jenny? We haven't heard from her in a while," Miss Jane said.

Jenny Simon, a.k.a. 1940s film starlet Jeannette Simone, was Mr. Riley's ex-wife and still good friend. While she lived here for a few months the year before, we'd discovered she had a daughter by Miss Aggie's older brother, Forrest Pennington. Jack had adopted the child, and no one knew who the real father was. I still got confused trying to untangle all the threads in that skein.

"Jenny is wonderful. She recently moved to Berlin so she could be near Helen and Samantha. I must admit, I find it very comforting to have her there."

I curled up in an oversized chair and tried to focus on the stories the octogenarian was relating. The seniors, including Martin, seemed mesmerized.

"So you hid on the train?" Frank's voice held admiration and incredulity.

Jack nodded, a faraway look in his eyes. "At one of the stops, I managed to slip off. I found the underground unit I was searching for and told them about the trainload of Jews being transported. I hoped they'd be able to do something, and they did their best. They managed to get the train stopped, killing most of the SS guards. The prisoners were all freed and scattered to the nearby woods." He paused, and pain clouded his eyes. "We later heard they'd all been rounded up and sent to the camp on the next train."

"Did any of them survive?" My voice sounded strange, and I shivered, wrapping my arms around my shoulders.

"From the information we received, everyone was sent to the gas chambers." He spoke quietly, and I wondered how he could tell such a story with no emotion. Then I saw his eyes and inhaled sharply. Oh yes, he felt emotion. Grief lay deep in those piercing eyes.

But if he was grieving, that knocked down my suspicions that he'd swindled wealthy European Jews of their property. Unless, of course, he'd come to regret it later. A wave of *déjà vu* washed over me, and I knew why. I'd been around this circle of thoughts before, the last time Jack Riley was here. I was determined, this time, to resolve the issue.

CHAPTER SEVEN

Miss Jane's black monster careened wildly around the sharp curves while I held tightly to the seat on the passenger side. I should've had my head examined. Why in the world had I agreed to let her drive to Caffee Springs?

"Jane! Please be careful." The terrified screech from the backseat was evidence enough that Miss Georgina felt the same.

"I'm being careful. Don't be such a scaredy-cat, Georgina."

Since the weather had warmed back up the last few days, we'd decided to drive over and try the new tearoom for lunch today. We all needed to get away from the constant reminder of the two-week-old murder.

The tires squealed as Miss Jane pulled into the sparse parking area at the side of the tearoom. We got out on wobbly legs. That is, mine. Miss Georgina's were wobbly, too. Miss Jane's confidence in her driving skills never ceased to amaze me.

A sign over the door of the light blue and white building read YE OLDE TEA SHOPPE.

"Why, what a lovely name," Miss Georgina said, with true amazement in her voice.

Miss Jane made an insulting sound with her teeth. "Not very original."

I had to agree, but as we went inside, the scent of cinnamon, vanilla, and other spices wafted across the room. The atmosphere was charming enough that the overused name could be forgiven.

The hostess, attired in a ruffled cap and apron, ushered us to a small round table, covered with a lace-trimmed cloth.

We scanned the small menu, and when the waitress arrived, we ordered soup, sandwiches, and a pot of tea.

After promising to be back with our drinks, she left the table. Georgina leaned forward. "How are your wedding plans going, dear?"

I sighed. "Oh, we're so far behind in our planning. I'm starting to think we'll never get everything done on time."

"Well, for goodness' sake, Victoria, why didn't you ask for help?" Miss Jane frowned and looked almost insulted.

"Thanks, Miss Jane. I'm sure I'll need your help when the day gets closer, but there are things Benjamin and I need to discuss and take care of."

"What's the holdup?" With her usual no-nonsense approach, Miss Jane had gotten right to the point.

"It seems every time we try to get together for an hour or two, something comes up."

"Dear, you're just going to have to make it a priority. Plan a time, and don't allow *anything* to interfere." With an emphatic nod, she turned and smiled at the waitress, who'd brought our tea and soup. When she put my bowl in front of me, the aroma of the tomato and spinach set my saliva glands working ahead of time. I wasted no time getting down to business.

At just the right moment, our sandwiches arrived.

"Oh dear, are these sprouts?" Miss Georgina asked. "I hate sprouts."

"Here, I think they switched them," I said, holding my plate out to her. "The one I ordered had sprouts. This one must be yours."

Gratefully, she accepted her toasted ham and cheese while I retrieved my chicken pecan salad on a whole wheat roll with loads of sprouts.

My back was to the door, but when the bell tinkled and I heard Miss Georgina gasp, I glanced over my shoulder to see who had entered.

"Why, it's Aggie and Mr. Riley." Miss Jane waved in their direction.

Mr. Riley waved back, and with a nod to the waitress, guided Miss Aggie to our table. He grabbed a nearby chair, and they joined us. Miss Aggie didn't appear too happy to see us, but I didn't think she'd be rude in front of Mr. Riley.

"What are you two doing here?" Miss Jane beamed at them.

"We're here to eat lunch, Jane." Sarcasm dripped from Miss Aggie's lips.

Wrong again, Victoria.

Miss Jane turned her attention to her tuna sandwich. Miss Aggie was the only one who could hurt her feelings. She'd practically been Miss Aggie's shadow when they were young and still seemed to need her approval.

"Miss Brody, I hope while I'm in Cedar Chapel I'll get a chance to taste your fabulous apple dumplings."

Way to go, Jack Riley.

Miss Jane brightened. "I'd be happy to make some for you. Next time you come to dinner."

He grinned. "I hope that means I can expect another dinner invitation. I do enjoy the company at Cedar Lodge."

"Of course, Mr. Riley. How about Sunday, after church?"

That would give me a chance to watch him and listen to his stories and perhaps catch a discrepancy somewhere. Oh dear, there I went again with my suspicions.

"Thank you, Miss Storm. I'll be there. Can I bring anything?" Oh so charming.

"Only yourself." I could charm, too.

When Miss Jane, Miss Georgina, and I had finished our lunch, we excused ourselves and left. Obviously the other two had gone out alone for a reason. And I needed to stop being so suspicious. After all, they shared an interest in Samantha.

We headed out of town, and Miss Jane took the back way to Cedar Chapel instead of the main highway.

I had a pretty good idea why.

As we drew near the private road that led up to Pennington House, Miss Jane slowed.

"Jane, what are you doing?" Miss Georgina's voice held an impatient whine.

"Oh, I thought with Aggie in Caffee Springs for a while, maybe we could take a peek at Pennington House."

"Now, Miss Jane. You know Miss Aggie wants us to wait until the opening so we'll be surprised."

"Oh, all right. But I think it's silly. A hotel is a hotel. And a restaurant is a restaurant. What's the big secret?'

She sped up but looked longingly up the hill as we passed the road.

When we got back to the lodge, Mabel met us at the kitchen door.

"Bobby is bringing my little Sarah this weekend. I'm so excited."

"Wonderful. When will you bring her to meet us?" I smiled at the happiness in her eyes.

"Bobby's going to enroll her in school Monday, and she'll ride the bus over here afterwards. Are you sure you don't mind?" She tossed me a worried glance.

"Of course I'm sure. It'll be nice to have a child here." I said it with more conviction than I actually felt. But the alternative was to lose Mabel, and that simply wouldn't do.

Miss Georgina and Miss Jane headed up to their rooms to nap. Buster followed at my side and nudged my hand as I headed for my office. "What is it, boy? Cabin fever?"

Buster smiled. Okay, I know dogs don't smile. But mine does.

I reached down and scratched him behind the ear. "I could use a walk, too."

At the word "walk," Buster raced back into the kitchen and began tugging at his leash. I grabbed it before he could pull the hook from the wall and snapped it to his collar.

Hoping to avoid Mrs. Miller, I headed in the other direction toward the park. There was only a scattering of people there, and they waved and went about their own business. With Buster running beside me, I jogged around the half-mile track, then did another round.

Breathing heavily, I flopped down on a bench. How did I get so out of shape? I used to run five miles every morning. Of course, that was past tense. Surprise struck me. It had been nearly two years since I'd exercised on a regular basis. Occasionally the seniors and I visited the fitness center, but most of the time I spent the whole hour in the hot tub. Well, that would change. I didn't really have time to go to the fitness center every day. Maybe I should buy a treadmill. Then I could jog when I had a half hour or so to spare.

Of course, treadmills were expensive. I weighed the pros and cons. My health won.

The afternoon sun warmed me, and I yawned. "C'mon, Buster. Can't go to sleep on a park bench. It would be just like Bob Turner to arrest me."

Miss Aggie pulled into the garage at the same time we got back to the lodge. I waved, then took Buster to the fenced backyard and removed his leash.

I followed Miss Aggie inside. "Did you enjoy your lunch with Mr. Riley?"

"I guess." She shoved past me and went upstairs.

Now what was wrong with her? I hoped she wasn't ill. I stood in the foyer, not sure what to do. Sometimes I had to walk on eggshells where Miss Aggie was concerned. I didn't want to intrude, but if she was ill, I needed to know.

I went upstairs and tapped on her door.

"Come in."

The fragrance of Chanel No. 5 wafted to my nostrils as I entered the room. At one time, the only concession Miss Aggie made to her wealth. Boy, had that ever changed.

She stood beside her bed, cramming piles of clothing in her suitcase. Silk blouses spilled over the sides, and a mink stole sprawled over the top of everything.

"Miss Aggie, where are you going?"

"I'm going to Jefferson City to stay with Simon for a while." Her nephew, Simon, was Corky's father.

"Oh. Is anything wrong? You're not worried about something, are you?" The last time she took off for Simon's on the spur of the moment was when an unknown man had been murdered at Pennington House, and she thought she was a target, too. Could this have something to do with Clyde's death?

She slammed the bag closed and locked it, then whirled around, her diamond earrings sparkling, and looked me in the eye.

"Can't I go visit my nephew without you meddling? I'm not a child, Victoria."

"Of course. I'm so sorry. I didn't mean to offend you."

Her expression softened. "It's all right. I know you mean well."

"Could you wait until morning? It's a little late to start out. It'll be dark before you get there."

She glared without answering and started to lift the suitcase off the bed.

I reached over and took it from her. "At least let me carry this for you. It's heavy."

After I put the suitcase in the trunk of her Lexus, she turned to me. "Don't worry, I'll be fine. I'll call when I get there."

As she drove away, a feeling of dread washed over me, but I shrugged and shook it off. Miss Aggie had driven herself to Jefferson City several times. She'd be fine.

⊗

The grandfather clock in the great hall chimed eight, the last echo resounding throughout the room. I tapped on the table by my chair. Why hadn't she called? Surely she was at Simon's by now. Should I call? She'd be furious. Maybe I'd give her another half hour or so.

I curled my legs up and leaned back, my eyes going to the portrait over the empty fireplace. His eyes seemed to stare into mine as though expecting something. I shivered. When was I going to learn to control my overactive imagination?

The unease I'd felt when Miss Aggie drove away hit me again. Harder this time. My heart raced. I jumped up. Enough was enough.

I went to my office and called Simon Pennington's residence. After the fourth ring, a breathless female answered.

"Pennington's. Lauren speaking." Simon's youngest daughter. She had a friendly lilt to her voice. Someday I'd like to meet this young lady.

"Miss Pennington, this is Victoria Storm at Cedar Lodge Boarding House in Cedar Chapel."

"Oh, hello Miss Storm. How is everything with Aunt Aggie?"

Oh no.

"She isn't there?" I couldn't control the shaking of my voice.

"No, Mom and Dad are on a cruise with friends from our church. Why would you think she was here?"

A chill washed over me, and my throat tightened so that I couldn't speak.

"Miss Storm? Are you there?"

I swallowed. "Yes, yes, I'm here. But I don't know what to think. Miss Aggie left here this afternoon. She said she was going there. Perhaps she didn't know your parents were gone."

"Oh, but she did. Father called her before they left. Whatever was she thinking?" Worry tinged her voice. "Do you think she might have had a memory lapse?"

"I don't know. She's not usually forgetful. But, of course, it's possible." I had no idea what Miss Aggie was up to, but I didn't think for a moment that she had forgotten Simon was on a cruise.

"I'm going to hang up and call Corky. If she shows up there or calls, will you please let me know?"

"Yes, of course. And please call me if you hear anything."

We said good-bye, and I hung up, immediately dialing Corky's number.

"Hello, Victoria." I heard music in the background.

"Corky, can you get over here?"

"What's up? Phoebe and I are at a show in Branson."

"Miss Aggie left today and said she was going to your parents' house in Jefferson City."

He laughed. "You must have misunderstood her. My folks are on a cruise."

"I didn't misunderstand her. She packed her suitcase, told me she was going to Simon's, and took off driving. I just talked to Lauren. She isn't there."

For a moment all I heard was Corky's breathing. Then, "And she doesn't answer her phone?"

Realization slammed against me. "I forgot all about her cell phone. I'll try now."

"Call me back."

"I will." I slammed the phone down and searched

through my address book until I found the number. Miss Aggie's phone rang. On the fourth ring, it clicked over to an automated message. I left a message for her to call Corky or me and hung up, then dialed again. Still no answer.

Corky answered on the first ring.

"No answer. I tried a couple of times."

"Okay, I didn't get an answer either. We're leaving now. See you in a half hour."

"Should I call Bob Turner?" By now my hands were shaking so I could hardly hold the phone.

"Maybe you'd better."

With a heavy heart, I called the sheriff.

"What?" His voice boomed through the receiver. "What do you mean she's missing again?"

I explained the situation as calmly as I could.

"Aw, she probably stopped to get something to eat."

"But why would she go there in the first place when she knew her nephew was out of town?"

"Forgot. You know how old people are."

Anger started to rise. "Why don't you tell me, Sheriff? How are old people?"

"Oh, you know. They get forgetful sometimes."

"Miss Aggie is not forgetful. Something is wrong."

He sighed. "Okay, I'll be there in a few minutes."

I made a quick call to Benjamin to fill him in on the situation. When he promised to come right over, I hung up and faced my next move. How was I going to tell the seniors?

Frank and Miss Evalina were in their room, so I went there first. I tapped on the door, and after a moment Frank opened it.

"Frank, would you and Miss Evalina mind coming down to the parlor? I need to talk to everyone."

Miss Evalina came up behind him. Her sharp eyes scanned my face. "What's wrong?"

"Miss Aggie is missing," I whispered.

"What?" They spoke in unison.

"Isn't she at Simon's?" Miss Evalina asked.

"No, and what's more, she knew Simon and his wife were on a cruise. She lied to me, and I'm worried sick."

She stepped out in the hallway, and Frank followed. They went into the downstairs front parlor while I headed for the rec room.

Miss Jane and Miss Georgina sat at the card table playing dominoes. Martin, head back, snored on the sofa while a western played on the TV.

"Ladies, would one of you wake Martin? I need to talk to everyone in the parlor."

"What about? It's almost bedtime." Miss Jane frowned in my direction.

"I'm sorry. But it's important."

One by one they joined us in the parlor.

"I'm going to make tea. Benjamin should be here shortly. And Corky and Phoebe are coming, too." I attempted a smile. "Oh, and the sheriff is on his way."

Before anyone could object or start firing questions at me, I headed to the kitchen and put the kettle on.

Benjamin was the first to arrive, followed shortly afterward by Sheriff Turner and Deputy Lewis. I brought the tea cart into the parlor with tea, coffee, and cookies. Benjamin liked his coffee, and I couldn't see Bob Turner drinking tea.

"Okay Victoria, what's going on?" The sheriff frowned at me and took a huge bite of a chocolate chip cookie.

"Just what I told you on the phone. Miss Aggie packed her suitcase and left in her car this afternoon around three o'clock. She told me she was going to her nephew's house in Jefferson City. When I called about eight thirty, Simon Pennington's daughter told me her parents are on a cruise with friends from their church. And furthermore, that her Aunt Aggie was aware of that fact. I tried to reach Miss Aggie on her cell phone, but she didn't answer."

Miss Georgina gasped and clutched her chest.

"Aggie's missing?" Miss Jane whispered the words. Her face paled.

"I'm sorry for you to hear it this way."

The sheriff scratched his head. "Hmm. It shouldn't have taken her more than four hours even if she drove slowly like most elderly ladies. Course she could have stopped for dinner. But even so, she'd have been there before eight thirty. Now what can that woman be up to this time?"

"What is that supposed to mean, Bob Turner?" Miss Evalina turned her schoolteacher glare on him. "This is the second time Aggie's been missing, and the first time, if you'll remember, she was kidnapped and came near to being killed. As did we all."

If the situation hadn't been so serious, the sheriff's flaming face would have been comical.

"It was just a figure of speech, Miz Cordell. I assure you, I didn't mean anything derogatory to Miz Brown."

"That's Pennington-Brown, Bobby Turner," Miss Jane snapped, her glare almost as scathing as Miss Evalina's.

The sheriff swallowed hard. Then he stiffened, and his lips tightened. "I said I'm sorry. Now, let's drop it and get on with important things, such as why she lied to Victoria and where she really went."

"And why she isn't answering her phone." We all turned. Corky stood in the doorway, his cell phone in his hand and his strained face a picture of worry.

CHAPTER EIGHT

Corky took Phoebe's hand, and they walked over to the love seat by the empty fireplace.

The sheriff ran his hands through his hair and threw Corky a hopeful look.

"Pennington. Do you have any idea where your aunt might have gone?"

"I wish I did." Corky's face was pale, and worry shadowed his eyes. "She was at the work site for a couple of hours this morning, then left for an appointment. She never came back. Then Victoria called and said she left for Jefferson City and never got there."

"An appointment, eh?" Sheriff Turner scratched his ear. "Did she say what it was?"

"No, I'm not in the habit of asking Aunt Aggie where she's going or with whom."

"We know where she went, Bob." Miss Georgina loved to share information. "We saw her at the new tearoom in Caffee Springs."

Sheriff Turner turned an accusing eye on me. "Did you plan on telling me that?"

"Yes, I just hadn't gotten around to it yet." Actually, I'd

planned on waiting until I had a chance to talk to Jack Riley, but the sheriff didn't have to know that. Because the more I thought about it, the more I realized it was suspicious that Miss Aggie had flown out of the house so fast right after lunching with Jack.

Tom Lewis took a step in my direction. "How about getting around to it now?"

I glared at him in as intimidating a manner as I could muster. "Back up, Lewis. Like Miss Georgina said, we were having lunch at the tearoom when Miss Aggie came in."

Sheriff Turner motioned for Tom to stand back. I suppose he didn't want us getting into a power struggle.

"Alone?"

I should have known he'd ask. There went my opportunity to get to Mr. Riley first. "No, Jack Riley was with her."

A flicker of interest jumped into the sheriff's eyes. "Hmm. Okay. Thank you. Anything else I need to know?"

I shrugged. "I wish I knew more, but that's about it."

Miss Jane leaned forward. "What are you going to do, Bobby?"

He sighed. "Now, Miz Brody. Don't you worry. We'll find Miz Brown. . .er. . .Miz Pennington-Brown. Just leave it to us."

The seniors glanced around at each other. None of them had much confidence in the sheriff and his deputy. I hoped they'd keep their lips buttoned.

Martin snorted, and I threw a warning glance his way. We didn't need trouble with the law. He pressed his lips together. I breathed a sigh of relief as he walked over to the window and looked out.

The sheriff glanced around the room, his gaze resting briefly on each of us and finally landing on Benjamin. "Grant, what are you doing here?"

Benjamin laughed. "Uh, these are my friends, Sheriff. And in case you've forgotten, Vickie is my fiancée."

"Hmm. Okay, Ben, don't go printing anything in that paper of yours about this."

"I hadn't really planned to since there's nothing to print at the moment, but if I recall, Sheriff, there is a little something called freedom of the press."

"Yeah. . .well. . .if there's nothing else. . .guess we'll get to the office. It's too early to file a missing persons report, but I'll do what I can."

"But Sheriff, my wife is expecting me back home. I haven't had dinner yet." Tom Lewis's expression was comical. You'd think he'd starved for a month.

"It'll have to wait. We've got a woman missing, for crying out loud, Tom." He turned to me. "I'll need her driver's license and license plate number and anything else you can think of that might help. She's still got the silver Lexus, right?"

"That's right. And her suitcase is in the trunk." What else could I tell him? "Oh, she was wearing a blue silk pantsuit and navy blue shoes with one-inch heels."

He nodded and scribbled the information on his notepad. "If you think of anything else, give me a call."

The officers left.

I glanced around at the miserable faces of my friends. Silence was thick in the room. What could we say?

"What are we going to do?" Dear Miss Evalina. So quiet most of the time, but the first to stir us to action when someone we loved might be in danger.

"Does this seem chillingly familiar to anyone?" Miss Jane sat stiffly against the back of the wing chair. Miss Aggie had been her best friend through the years. I knew she must be worried sick.

I went over and put my arm around her thin shoulders. "Miss Jane. We found her before, and we'll find her again. After all, she knew her nephew was away, so apparently she was telling a fib when she said she was going there."

"But why would she do that? Why didn't she just say where she was going?" Miss Jane wailed. "Didn't she know we'd worry?"

Ben cleared his throat. "Maybe she planned to call you and forgot. After all, she had no way of knowing Victoria would call Simon's house." That was true, but Miss Aggie had promised to phone me when she arrived. "She's probably having a late dinner somewhere and will call soon and tell everyone off for causing a stir."

"I don't know." Corky's face was sober. "I can't imagine her going off somewhere when she was so gung ho about finishing up Pennington House."

"All right." Frank stood up. "There's no sense in sitting here stewing about it. This isn't solving anything."

"Frank's right." Miss Evalina stood, too. "I'm going upstairs. Let's each try to think about Aggie's actions today. Perhaps something will give us a clue as to what she's up to."

The two left and went up to their suite. I returned to the sofa and sat next to Benjamin.

"I don't know what to do." Corky looked as though he might wring his hands like Miss Georgina. Instead he took his phone from his pocket and punched in a number. He listened, then flipped it closed.

"Still no answer?" Phoebe's voice held sympathy, and she reached over and squeezed his hand.

He shook his head and got up. "Phoebe needs to eat. I guess we'll go to Hannah's."

"I could warm up something from dinner or make an omelet."

"Thanks, but I need to do something besides sit here and think about Aunt Aggie. If she calls you, please tell her to call me, too, okay?"

"Wait a minute, Corky." Miss Evalina touched his arm gently. "First, we need to do what we always do when one of us is in trouble. What we did when Aggie was missing before. Pray to the One who knows where she is and can bring her safely home."

A breath of relief rushed through me. "Thank you, Miss Evalina. We should have done that first. Frank, will you lead us in prayer?"

Everyone bowed their heads, and Frank uttered a heartfelt prayer.

Corky promised to call if he heard anything. They left, Phoebe's hand resting protectively on his arm. An unusual reversal in procedure. But this had to be especially difficult for Corky. It had been less than two years since his aunt's kidnapping. We hadn't known where she was then, either, and we'd all secretly suspected for a while that Corky was involved in some way with her disappearance.

I glanced at Benjamin, then at Miss Jane and Miss Georgina. I was afraid they'd be up until Miss Aggie called.

If she called. Martin sat in a chair next to Miss Georgina, and I caught his attention. He must have read my mind, because he jumped up.

"Okay ladies, there's no sense in us sitting here and letting our imaginations run wild. Aggie'll more than likely be calling anytime. What say we play dominoes or something while we wait?"

"Do you want to, Jane?" Miss Georgina asked.

Miss Jane sighed deeply and glanced up at her friend. "I guess we might as well. Martin's right. No sense in calling up trouble when it may not be there at all."

I stared after them as they left the room. I couldn't remember Miss Jane ever admitting Martin might be right about anything.

"Are you going to be all right, sweetheart?" Benjamin took my hand and lifted it to his lips. My hand tingled, and stress seemed to slide off me.

I smiled and rested my head on his shoulder. "I'm fine."

"Want to sit outside on the swing for a while?"

"Yes. That sounds wonderful." I hesitated. "But what if Miss Aggie calls?"

"We'll leave the door open so we can hear the phone."

I stacked cups and saucers on the tea cart, and Benjamin pushed it to the kitchen for me. I grabbed a couple of bottles of water from the refrigerator, and we went outside, leaving the front door open.

We sat on the swing in silence. The sky looked almost black tonight, with a field of bright stars. Almost like a Texas sky on a clear night. But not quite.

"What do you think, Victoria?"

I took a swig of water and gulped it down. What did I think? That Miss Aggie was simply on an innocent, if mysterious, excursion of some kind? Not for a minute. I'd finally put my finger on that disturbed feeling I'd had since Miss Aggie had pulled into the garage that afternoon. Her expression wasn't anger or impatience or any of the other emotions that played so easily on her face from time to time. The look was fear. Real fear. And mixed in with the fear was a determination that bothered me more than the fear. Whatever Miss Aggie was up to, I believed it had something to do with Clyde's death. And I was very much afraid she was stepping into danger.

⊂ଽ

After a sleepless night that left me with a throbbing headache, I called Lauren Pennington and found that she hadn't heard from Miss Aggie. I dressed and went downstairs. The aroma of coffee drew me to the dining room, where I found all the seniors around the table. Their hopeful eyes turned to me, and I shook my head. "I'm sorry. I haven't heard anything."

I went to the buffet, more to escape the dejected looks on their faces than anything. I probably couldn't eat a bite. I poured a mug of coffee and carried it to the table.

"Victoria, you need to eat something." Miss Jane went to the sideboard and filled a plate. Without a word, she set it down in front of me.

Sometimes it was nice having Grandma's old friends to mother me. Other times, such as now, it was a downright nuisance. I took a sip of coffee and ignored the steaming plate of bacon and eggs. Miss Jane ignored me ignoring the food.

The phone rang, cutting through the silence and penetrating my mind like a scream in the night.

I jumped up and rushed to grab the kitchen phone. "Miss Aggie, is that you?"

A sharp intake of breath came through the receiver. "I'm sorry, Victoria. This is Jack Riley."

"Mr. Riley. Do you know anything about Miss Aggie's disappearance?" I hadn't meant to blurt it out. I needed to calm down and start using wisdom.

"I'm sorry. I don't. Sheriff Turner talked to me this morning, and I knew if he suspected I was involved, you might, too. I wonder if you would meet me for coffee, so we can talk without the seniors around. I don't want to upset them by speaking of Aggie."

"Yes, do you mind if I bring Benjamin along?" I wasn't about to go anywhere alone with Jack Riley just yet.

"Of course. Bring anyone you like."

"Hannah's? Or the Mocha Java?"

"Is there someplace we can meet where we aren't as likely to run into friends and neighbors?"

Why hadn't I thought of that? "There's a new truck stop about five miles south of town. A lot of the townspeople went to check it out the first week or so, but I doubt we'd see any of them there. We're all pretty loyal to locals."

"What time would be best for you?"

"I'll need to check with Ben. Call me back in ten minutes?"

"Very well." I heard the click of the phone and punched in Benjamin's number.

"Good morning, my love."

I grinned. I really needed to get a phone with caller ID.

And, I reminded myself, a cell phone.

"Good morning," I crooned, then snapped out of it. I didn't have time to flirt with Benjamin this morning. "Listen, Jack Riley wants to have coffee for some reason. Are you free to go to the truck stop with me sometime today?"

"How about I pick you up around nine?" His voice was alert.

"Okay, I'll be ready."

After Mr. Riley called back, I returned to the dining room and told the seniors about his request.

"I'm going, too," Miss Jane stated. "If he knows something about Aggie, I want to be there."

"He says he doesn't know anything, Miss Jane," I reminded her.

"Jane, please go to the center with us," Miss Georgina pleaded. "Or maybe we should stay home in case she calls. What if she calls while you're gone, Victoria?"

"Mabel will be here. If Miss Aggie calls, she'll give her Benjamin's cell phone number."

Finally, Miss Jane agreed to go with the others, and they left after I promised to tell them every word of the conversation with Jack Riley.

I was waiting on the porch when Ben's truck pulled up in front. He got out and kissed me soundly before opening the passenger door for me. I reached up and pushed back a lock of his blond hair, still damp from the shower.

We left town and drove the few miles to the truck stop. Trucks were pulling out one after the other, and by the time we got inside, there were only a few customers scattered around the booths.

We glanced around. I didn't see Mr. Riley anywhere.

"Guess we beat him here," Benjamin said. "Let's take that back booth."

We ordered coffee and waited, looking up every time the door opened.

"I wonder what he wants to talk to us about." I'd been wondering ever since the man had called. Suddenly, my stomach growled.

"Did you eat breakfast?" Benjamin frowned.

"No, I wasn't hungry. Then when Mr. Riley called, I forgot all about food."

Benjamin signaled our waitress and asked for a menu.

I ended up ordering bacon and eggs. So much for ignoring Miss Jane.

I ate my breakfast and asked for a refill on my coffee. Mr. Riley still hadn't arrived.

"Benjamin, it's nearly ten. Where is he?" I was a little aggravated, and I didn't much care if it showed.

"Maybe he got held up. Do you know Phoebe's home phone number?"

"Yes, I do. Should we call?"

He pulled out his phone and flipped open the cover while I got my small address book out of my purse. I opened it to the Collinses' number and slid it across to Benjamin.

Before he had a chance to punch in the number, his phone rang.

"Hello. Grant here. Uh-huh. I see." He looked at me and mouthed "Riley." "That's quite all right, Mr. Riley. But can you give me an idea of what you wanted to speak to us about? I see. Yes. Good-bye."

"Was that him?"

"Yes, he's been called out of town." His forehead wrinkled in deep furrows.

"What? Why didn't he call us sooner?" The very nerve of the guy.

"He said he received an important call and couldn't get away to phone us sooner." He glanced at me. "I don't know, Vickie. Something doesn't seem right to me."

"Me either. What if he's done something to Miss Aggie and now he's skipping town?" My chest felt heavy, and dizziness washed over me. "Ben, we have to stop him."

"Honey, what's wrong?"

My head steadied, and I took a deep breath. "Let's go stop him before he gets away."

"Sweetheart, if he was skipping town, would he have announced it to us?"

I sat back. "I guess not. But it does seem suspicious to me. And you said yourself something seemed amiss."

He nodded. "Yes, but that doesn't mean I think he's harmed Miss Aggie."

I sighed. "We might as well leave."

He picked up the guest check from the table, and I followed him to the cash register. When we got back to the lodge, I said good-bye and promised to call him if I heard anything.

The house was quiet when I walked in, which was strange. Usually, at the least, I could hear pots rattling or Mabel singing. I walked into the kitchen.

Mabel stood beside the wall phone, the receiver in her hand. "That was the sheriff."

"What'd he want?"

"He wants you to call him." Eyes wide, she handed me the phone.

"Has something happened? Did they find Miss Aggie?"

"I don't know. He wouldn't tell me anything. But he didn't sound happy."

I punched in the number, and after two rings Tom Lewis picked up.

"Tom, this is Victoria Storm."

"Hold on. I'll transfer you to the sheriff. He wants to talk to you."

"Victoria?" Bob Turner's voice boomed over the wire. "Is that you?"

"Yes. Did you find Miss Aggie?"

"No, we didn't. But we found her car. I need you to come down to the office."

"What? Her car? Where?" *Oh, dear God, please.*

"Abandoned at the airport. Now don't get all riled up. I figure she changed her mind and decided to fly instead of drive. But not knowing exactly where she was going or even what airline she used, it may take awhile to find out for sure."

"But that doesn't make sense. She wouldn't just leave her car."

"Now, she might. Did you say she had a suitcase with her?"

"Yes, yes, I put it in the trunk for her. Is it still there?"

"No, it's gone, so that's a pretty good indication she wasn't nabbed or something."

"Have you told Corky?"

"Of course. He's her next of kin. At least around here. I called him first. He's coming to the office, too."

"Okay, I'll be there in a few minutes."

"Victoria." He cleared his throat. "Now don't go jumping to conclusions, but we did find something."

Get on with it. "What, Sheriff? What did you find?"

"Her cell phone. Seems she forgot to take it out of the car."

CHAPTER NINE

The seniors had to be told. I called the center and asked to speak to Frank. If anyone could keep the ladies from hysterics, it would be him.

"Frank, they've found Miss Aggie's car at the airport."

"At the airport? You mean just the car?" I knew the others must be close by, because he spoke little above a whisper.

"That's right. The sheriff is checking airlines to find out where she went, but this seems suspicious to me. Furthermore, she left her cell phone in the car. That's not like her at all."

"You're right. Her favorite toy. What are we going to do?"

"The sheriff wants me to come to his office. I'm not sure why. Do you want to meet me there?"

"Okay. We'll see you shortly." He hesitated. "Does Corky know?"

"Yes, he's probably at the courthouse by now."

I hung up, then punched in Benjamin's office number.

"Cedar Chapel Gazette."

I gritted my teeth at the sultry tone of Christiana's voice.

"I need to speak to Benjamin, please."

"I'm sorry. He's busy at the moment."

"What? Listen, this is Victoria Storm, and I need to speak with Benjamin *now*."

"I'm so sorry, Miss Storm. But, as I said, Benjamin is occupied at the moment."

I slammed down the phone and punched in his cell number, wondering why I hadn't done that in the first place.

He answered on the first ring. "Hi, sweetheart."

There was no time to complain about his secretary, so I quickly told him the news.

A low whistle came through the receiver. "Now Victoria, don't jump to conclusions. You know Miss Aggie. She probably decided to fly off somewhere on a whim."

"I wish everyone would stop telling me not to jump to conclusions. Benjamin, I'm worried. First, she lies and says she's going to Simon's; then she abandons her car and cell phone. That's not like her."

"All right, honey. Do you want me to drive you to the courthouse, or should I meet you there?"

"Aren't you busy?"

"It can wait."

"No, no. I think he just wants us to identify the cell phone or something. You don't have to leave work."

"All right, if you're sure, but call me when you get back to the lodge."

"I will. Bye."

I looked up to see Mabel eyeing me with a worried expression.

"What's wrong?"

"I need to leave at noon. This is the day Bobby is bringing my little Sarah."

"Oh Mabel, I forgot this was your afternoon off. That's fine. You go ahead."

"There's a pot of soup to warm for lunch, and I'll make a tray of sandwiches to go with it. Dinner is in the slow cooker, and there's a salad in the refrigerator."

"Thank you. I'll see you Monday."

"If you need me, call. I'll come. Bobby and Sarah will just have to understand."

I gave her a hug. "Okay, but I'm sure that won't be necessary."

I grabbed my keys and went to the garage.

Thoughts battered at my mind as I drove to the courthouse. What if something terrible had happened to Miss Aggie? It had happened before. And maybe this was connected in some way with Clyde's murder and the scrap of paper we found. After all, the emeralds were still missing, and who knew what else? Renovations and decorating were almost finished, and Miss Aggie would be moving into the old house soon. Could someone think she had the information they wanted? Or could they be afraid she'd find what they were looking for? After all, she was the rightful owner of the emeralds. That is, if they were legal.

I turned onto the square and parked in front of the courthouse. Frank and Miss Evalina sat in their car, and Miss Jane and Georgina were there in Miss Jane's Cadillac. Martin's new Dodge pickup pulled in next to them.

Tom Lewis groaned as we all walked in together. Had he really thought I'd leave the seniors out of this? They'd all been friends many years before my parents were born, much less me. And no matter how aggravated they might get at Miss Aggie, she was still one of them. Her memories were their memories. There was a bond there. And they deserved our respect.

Ready to stand against Tom's objections, I was surprised when he motioned for us all to go back to the sheriff's private office.

Sheriff Turner stood up as we walked in. He didn't look surprised to see the seniors, which was probably why Tom hadn't objected, except for the groan.

"Tom, bring more chairs in here." He left the door open and ushered the three senior ladies to the chairs that were available, including his own, which he pulled from behind the desk. When Tom had brought more, placing one behind the sheriff's desk, we all sat.

"Isn't Corky here yet?" I asked, glancing around the room.

"Pennington's been here and left. He told me to let you know he's filled out a missing person's report for Miz Pennington-Brown, and he'll be over to the lodge as soon as he can get away from Pennington House."

"All right Bob, now what's going on about Aggie? She wouldn't have gotten on an airplane. She loved that Lexus too much." Miss Jane eyed the sheriff like she thought he was trying to pull a fast one.

"Now Miz Brody, we can't be sure of that. She might have wanted to go someplace too far for her to drive."

"She used to say she'd like to see the Amazon," Miss Georgina piped up.

Martin and Frank both snorted, the snorts accompanied by one that came clearly through the door from Tom Lewis.

Miss Georgina's face flamed. "She did say that."

"That's right, she did." Miss Evalina glared at Frank and

Martin. "I've heard her say it, too, Georgina."

"And so have I," Miss Jane said. "But. . .Aggie hasn't gone to the Amazon."

The sheriff threw me a pleading glance.

"All right, we all need to listen to Sheriff Turner now." I let my smile take all of them in and was relieved to see them relax a little. They could just as easily have gotten upset with me. "So, have you had any luck finding her on any of the flights?"

"Er, not yet." He frowned and averted his eyes. "But they're still looking."

I pressed my lips together. They'd have found out by now if Miss Aggie had been on any of the flights that day.

The sheriff gave me a nervous glance, then rubbed his hands together. "Now, the reason I asked Victoria to come down was to identify the cell phone and a few other items we found in the car."

"There was more than the cell phone?" He hadn't mentioned that on the phone.

He ignored me and glanced around. "Pennington identified the phone but wanted to get a second opinion on the other items."

I tensed. Aggie seldom left anything in her car. "What items, Sheriff?"

He stepped over to his file cabinet and unlocked one of the drawers. The minute he opened it, I could smell Chanel No. 5. He sat back down and put a small box on his desk.

"We found these items in and around the car." He pulled out a capless perfume bottle. "This was next to the car. As you can see, the top is broken. The lid must have rolled away.

We didn't find it."

"That's Aggie's." Miss Jane's voice was low.

"We figure it fell out of her purse. I know how ladies are about leaving purses unfastened." He grinned.

"Aggie would never have left her handbag open. She was too afraid of robbery." Miss Evaline's statement was true, especially since the kidnapping.

Sheriff Turner cleared his throat. "Uh, yes, and this here pearl bracelet. The clasp is broken. We found it on the floorboard. It probably fell off, and she didn't know it."

The ladies and I all gasped.

"No, Sheriff," I protested. "There's no way Miss Aggie would have been that careless with her pearl bracelet. Or any of her jewelry for that matter."

"Victoria's right." Miss Evalina spoke for the first time. "There's some sort of foul play here, Sheriff."

"Now, now, ladies, don't get all riled up. She was probably late for her flight and didn't notice the bracelet."

"But. . ." Before Miss Georgina could say more, Miss Evalina reached over and touched her arm, silencing her.

We needed to get out of there and talk this over. "The items you've shown us are Miss Aggie's. Is there anything else you need from us, Sheriff?"

"Er. . .no, I guess not. You can go."

We stood and left the room, mute.

Once outside, the roar started as everyone began to talk at once. Passersby were gawking.

"Wait," I said, holding my hand up. "Let's go back to the lodge where we can talk privately."

Miss Jane sent me a scathing look. "I want to know where

Aggie is. And I don't think we're going to find her by talking."

"Now Jane, Victoria's right. We need to put our heads together and see what we can think of to do." Bless Miss Evalina's voice of reason.

"Besides, it's getting cold out here." Miss Georgina shivered.

She was right. I pulled my sweater tighter around me and noticed the others doing the same.

We piled into our vehicles and headed for home with Miss Jane's black Cadillac leading the way. I hoped we didn't look like a funeral procession.

CB

October was making a grand entrance in Cedar Chapel. By the time we arrived back at the lodge, the temperature had dropped into the thirties, and the wind whipped around the building with a roar, making me thankful my grandfather had added an attached garage to the house. I tried not to think about Buster's walk.

We were welcomed home by the heavenly aroma of Mabel's wonderful beef noodle soup and hot coffee. She'd heated up the soup and left it on the warmer for us. The seniors had left the center before lunch was served, so they were all hungry. My own stomach was making its needs known to me as well. We quickly washed up, and Miss Jane helped me get the soup and sandwiches into the dining room where Mabel had left dishes and flatware on the sideboard. There was also a container of cookies for dessert.

By common consent, we ate our lunch without mentioning Miss Aggie's disappearance. After we'd cleared the table and loaded the dishwasher, Miss Jane joined the others in the front parlor while I called Benjamin and filled him in on the latest news. He promised to be over in a half hour or so. Relieved that he was coming, I went to the parlor.

Logs in the fireplace crackled and popped as flames leaped around them, and the welcomed smell of wood smoke greeted me.

"Oh wonderful. Who do I thank for getting the fire going?"

"I brought the wood in, and Frank stacked it up and lit the match," Martin said with a grin.

"Then, thank you both." I smiled at Martin, who usually didn't volunteer to do much.

We settled ourselves in the chairs and sofas. Frank and Miss Evalina claimed the love seat, and I curled up in my favorite overstuffed chair.

"What do you think is going on, Victoria?" Frank was direct, as usual.

"I'm not sure, but I don't believe for a minute Miss Aggie boarded a plane. They'd have a record of it, and the sheriff would know by now."

The doorbell rang, and when I went to the door, it was Corky. He looked tired, and the worry in his eyes spoke volumes. He followed me to the parlor and flopped down in the chair next to mine.

"I'm sure the sheriff showed you the perfume bottle and bracelet. They're Aunt Aggie's, aren't they?"

I nodded, and the slight hope in his eyes faded. I reached over and patted his hand.

"I don't understand who would want to kidnap her," he said, raking his fingers through his hair.

Miss Georgina gasped. "Kidnapped? Oh no. Not again. She couldn't have been kidnapped again, could she, Victoria?"

"Georgina, calm down, please." Miss Evalina, seated between Miss Georgina and Frank, put her arm around her friend's plump shoulder. "We don't know that Aggie has been abducted. She's probably gone off somewhere without even thinking we might be worried." But her eyes said she didn't believe her own words.

Miss Jane's face was strained, and for the first time, she looked her eighty two years.

By the time Benjamin arrived, we'd come up with nothing helpful.

"This room is starting to depress me." Miss Georgina's words didn't surprise me. We did seem to discuss a lot of trouble in this parlor. But we'd come up with plenty of solutions, too.

This time, however, solutions eluded us, and by the time Ben and Corky left, we'd come no closer to an explanation for Miss Aggie's car and belongings.

The afternoon seemed to drag on forever, and the house was nearly silent as we each dealt with the latest shock.

Somehow, we managed to eat dinner. I did the cleanup alone, preferring to be left with my thoughts. The seniors went to bed early. I was sure they were all exhausted from the stress. I was feeling it myself.

There must be something we could do. I went to my office and pulled up the document with my lists.

My eyes came to rest on Clyde's entry. The more I looked at it, the stronger the feeling grew. Miss Aggie's disappearance had something to do with Clyde and/or the treasure. I glanced at my watch. Only nine. It wasn't too late to call Laura Baker. I grabbed the phone and dialed her hotel.

"Yes, Miss Storm, what can I do for you?"

"Would it be possible for us to meet again? I have some things I'd like to discuss."

She agreed, and we made an appointment to meet at the steak house in Caffee Springs for lunch the next day.

Feeling relieved just to have done something, I headed up to bed. As I passed Miss Aggie's room, sorrow washed over me and tears flooded my eyes. "We'll find you, Miss Aggie," I whispered. "I promise we'll find you."

ᴄ

I followed the hostess to a booth near the rear of the restaurant, wood chips scattering beneath my feet. Surprised and annoyed to see Christiana seated next to her mother, I slid into the padded seat on the other side of the table.

"I hope you don't mind me tagging along, Victoria. When Mother told me she was meeting you for lunch, I decided to join you."

"Not at all. You're welcome, of course," I lied.

The waiter took our orders then brought our drinks to the table. We sipped iced tea, and I wondered what to do. I'd planned on opening up to Laura about Miss Aggie's suspicions concerning Clyde and shady dealings, but I wasn't sure if I should in front of Christiana.

"What did you want to talk to Mom about?" Christiana's voice was challenging, but her dark eyes were intense and waiting.

I smiled. If she thought she could intimidate me, she had another think coming.

"Tiana, don't be rude." Laura bit her lip and threw me an apologetic smile.

"That's quite all right, Laura. We can talk another time." I glanced at Christiana to see her reaction.

She didn't disappoint me. "You mean you don't want to talk in front of me? What do you have to hide?"

"Why, not a thing. It just happens my business is with your mother, and it's private." I directed an oh-so-sweet smile straight at her.

A blush tinged her tan face, and her eyes flashed with anger. She jumped up. "Fine. I have to get back to the office anyway."

"But Tiana, you haven't had lunch yet. And you've ordered." The dismay in Laura's voice made me almost wish I'd gone ahead and discussed things in front of her daughter.

The girl flashed a smile my way. "Actually, I'd forgotten. Benjamin asked me to have a late lunch with him today."

Was that a truck that hit me in the stomach? I took a deep breath, determined not to show any reaction to her words. She was probably lying anyway, just to get under my skin.

"That's nice. Benjamin has always been thoughtful of his office staff." There. That should prove to her I was all right with her having lunch with my fiancé. "He tells me you're doing a great job."

"Really? He's never mentioned you at all to me." With a toss of her head, she left.

Her mother's sigh caught my attention.

"Please forgive her manners. She's young, and I'm afraid my mother rather spoiled her. Mom lived with us for years after my divorce." Sadness filled her eyes. "She passed away last year. Tiana misses her a lot."

"I understand. Please don't worry about it. I'm afraid I may have goaded her a little." I knew I had.

"By the way, she fibbed. Benjamin told us all about you at our first meeting with him. She knows very well you're getting married in December."

Relief rippled through me. Of course I knew Benjamin loved me, but still. . . . I sighed. I thought I'd gotten over being jilted by my former fiancé. My goodness, it had been several years. But apparently I still had issues to deal with.

The waiter brought our food, and we ignored Tiana's entrée as we ate.

When the waiter picked up our dishes, he looked pointedly at the untouched plate of food.

Laura smiled and asked for a to-go box. We ordered coffee and leaned back.

"Oh, by the way, Victoria, did you know the sheriff has released my father's property to me?"

"Are you serious?" I'd thought he'd tighten things up more with Miss Aggie missing.

"Yes, he said it's been thoroughly combed for evidence."

Excitement coursed through me. This was going to be easier than I'd thought. "Would you mind if I do another search? I still feel there's something there."

"But wouldn't the sheriff have found any evidence?"

I held my tongue for a moment, not wanting to say anything to make the sheriff sound stupid. "You're probably right. But I'd feel more comfortable if I could look things over once more."

"I don't mind, but you'd better do it soon. I'm putting the shop up for sale."

CHAPTER ▮▮ ▮▮▮ TEN

The cold wind lashed around me as I got out of the van in front of Clyde's store on Monday morning. Dark clouds threatened rain. Probably soon. All I needed. Cold rain. I suppressed a sigh. At least the temperature was above freezing, whether it felt like it or not.

Laura had given me a key in case I arrived before she did. A good thing, because there was no sign of her car, and the shop was dark.

I put the key in the lock and turned.

"What exactly do you think you're up to now, Victoria Storm?"

I groaned and slowly turned to face the sheriff. Anger reddened his face, and his teeth were clenched. I held up the key.

"Oh, so now you've managed to get your hands on a key. How'd you pull that off?"

Indignant, I opened my mouth.

"Never mind handing me a bunch of lies." He shook his finger in front of my nose. "Give me that key, and get on out of here."

Laura's blue SUV pulled up. She parked and jumped

out. "It's all right, Sheriff. Miss Storm and I arranged to meet here today to look over furniture. I gave her my spare key in case she got here first, and it appears she did."

The sheriff looked from me to Laura, a cloud of suspicion in his eyes. "Furniture, huh?"

"That's right. She's thinking of purchasing a few pieces for her boardinghouse."

Wow, what a liar. I tried not to look surprised. How would I get out of this if Bob Turner directed his questions to me? After all, Laura wasn't a Christian, so she probably thought it was a justified fib. I knew I couldn't get by with such a thing. My conscience would hurt too much. As a matter of fact, it was hurting even as I stood there in silence. Should I tell the sheriff it wasn't so? But then Laura would look bad.

He squinted at us, his fingers tapping against his thigh. Finally, he nodded and got back in the squad car. I bit my lip as he pulled away.

Laura laughed, and then as she turned and saw my expression, she frowned. "What's the matter?"

"I suppose I was surprised you felt it necessary to make up a story. We had a perfect right to be here."

She shrugged. "I suppose so. But he'd have hung around longer. What difference does it make?"

Suppressing the answer that rose up in me, I followed her into the shop. A cacophony of barks, meows, chirps and a myriad of other animal sounds greeted us. From the din, I suspected the elderly lady who was supposed to be feeding them hadn't arrived yet.

"What in the world am I going to do with all these creatures?" Laura looked around, obviously overwhelmed.

"You might call the pet stores in neighboring towns and let them know you've closed the business and have animals and other merchandise to sell."

"Good idea. Thanks. My father left very few assets, so any money I can bring in will help."

I glanced at her expensive coat and the name-brand pant-suit she was wearing. Surely she wasn't hurting for money.

She noticed my glance. "You see. . ." She stopped and cleared her throat. "Miss Storm, I'm going to go through these papers from my father's safe-deposit box while you look around. Just make yourself at home."

Safe-deposit box? Interesting. If Clyde wanted to hide something, what better place? But how could I find out what was in there? Ask?

"So, I'll be in the office if you need me for anything." Laura walked through the door to the back room while I mentally kicked myself. Of course I couldn't ask what was in Clyde's safe-deposit box. What was I thinking?

I ran up the stairs and looked around the small apartment, not sure where to begin. We'd gone through every inch of it before, and I was sure the sheriff had, too. It was silly to even think we might have missed something. I went to the small bedroom and checked all the bedknobs on the four-poster. Then went through every inch of every drawer, even checking the bottoms of the furniture to see if something might be taped there.

After an hour of useless searching, I went downstairs.

I tapped on the office door and walked in. Startled, Laura looked up, her cheeks flushed and excitement in her eyes. She slid a large envelope on top of the papers she'd been perusing.

"Oh, Miss Storm." She sounded breathless. "Did you find anything?"

"No, nothing at all." I couldn't help my eyes from wandering to the papers. "How about you? Anything interesting in the box?" There, I'd asked anyway.

"N–no. Just some old letters," she said, her eyes evading mine.

"Okay, then I'll get back to the lodge. Thank you for letting me look around."

I left the shop, my mind darting to the letters from Clyde's box. Laura was definitely hiding something. Was it possible she knew more about this case than she was admitting? Even something about Clyde's murder?

ɔ℘

I decided to swing by the Mocha Java for a latte, but when I passed Hannah's, I noticed Benjamin's Avalanche parked in front. So I pulled into the parking spot next to it. I pushed through the door, waving at Hannah, who motioned toward the back. I turned with a grin and headed that way, then stopped, the grin frozen on my face.

Benjamin sat in a booth next to the window, with Christiana perched—an enormous smile on her face—right next to him. Just like a cat that had stolen the cream.

I focused on Benjamin's face. Did he look pleased? Happy? Hmm. He actually looked downright uncomfortable. Okay. I could handle this. I relaxed the grin that had taken residence on my lips and started toward the booth. As I drew near, Christiana glanced up and saw me. Instead of the embarrassment or fear that should have shown on her face, the little floozy gave me a taunting smile.

"Hi," I purred. "Who's minding the store?"

Benjamin gulped. Yes, he gulped. Then he cleared his throat. "Jory's there. Christiana has an appointment later." Jory had worked for Ben for ages. He was the all around fix it man and knew everything about the newspaper business.

I looked pointedly at Christiana. Slowly, she unfolded her body from the vinyl seat. She smiled slowly at Benjamin as though they shared a secret. "I need to meet Mother at the courthouse. See you later, Benjamin."

She brushed past me without a word.

"Sit down, Victoria. People are looking." He patted the seat next to him.

I sat on the other side and glared across at him, waiting to see how he'd get out of this one.

"Don't look at me like that. I'm an innocent man." He grinned, reached over, and tried to take my hand, which I slid out of the way.

"Yes, it looked that way."

"Okay, this is what happened." He took a deep breath. "I came in about fifteen minutes ago to get a cup of coffee and try to round up some local news. Tiana came in and sat by me. I didn't invite her. In fact, I was about to suggest she move to the other seat when you walked in. That's it."

"Okay."

"Okay?"

"Yes, I believe you. But you need to keep your guard up,

because that girl is out to get you."

Annoyance crossed his face. "Don't be silly, Victoria. She's just a kid."

"No, she is not a kid. She knows very well what she wants, and she wants you."

"I thought you said you weren't jealous." He wrinkled his brow several times, causing his eyebrows to go up and down. Was he mocking me?

I felt something like hot lava rising in me. How dare he!

"For your information, I am not jealous. I just happen to know what she's up to. And you're too naïve to see. Or maybe you do see, but you're enjoying it too much to admit it." When I realized I was shaking my finger in front of his face, I put my hand down.

"Now wait a minute." He'd raised his voice, and several people were looking our way.

"I don't believe I will. I'm going home."

"Vickie." He started to rise.

I stormed out of the café and got into the van. Out of the corner of my eye, I saw Benjamin standing in the open door with his hand raised. I peeled out. *Take that*, I thought.

I was almost home before regret hit me. I knew I'd acted foolishly, because in my heart I believed Ben. It just made me so mad he couldn't see what the little vixen was up to. I sighed. Maybe I'd call him.

I parked in the driveway and went in the front door. When I stepped into the foyer, I heard Mabel's strong voice singing "The Old Rugged Cross." I hung my coat in the hall closet and tried to calm down before I walked into the kitchen.

"You sound happy today, Mabel." I smiled as she pounded

a piece of meat on a hard plastic cutting board. "How did your weekend go?"

"Great, just great." She brought the metal meat pounder down once more then began cutting it into pieces. "Bobby's getting Sarah enrolled this morning, and then he's headed home."

"She knows where to get off the bus?"

"Yes, but if it's all right with you, I'll take a minute and walk down to the corner when it's time. Just this first day."

"Of course. You know I don't mind. What are you making?" Sometimes I gave her a menu, but most of the time I let her fix whatever she wanted. She hadn't disappointed me yet.

"Beef and noodles. Found a new recipe with sour cream. Thought you might like it." She grinned. She knew I liked most anything with sour cream.

"Sounds wonderful. I need to work in my office for a couple of hours. I'll just have a small chef salad for lunch, if you don't mind."

"Don't mind a bit."

I filled a mug with coffee and carried it into the office. I set it on the coaster that rested on my desk and sat in the padded swivel chair, wondering if it was too soon to call Benjamin.

Just as I reached for the phone, it rang. "Cedar Chapel Lodge."

"Hi, sweetheart. Are you still mad?" Benjamin's voice sounded half teasing, half worried.

"No, I'm not mad."

"Good. Honey, I got to thinking, you may be right. I

don't see it, but I promise I'll be watchful, and if I see any indication you're right, I'll let her go."

Any indication? Men were so gullible where pretty girls were concerned.

"It's okay, Ben. I'm watching her, too." I didn't know whether to laugh or cry, so I did neither. "Would you like to come to dinner tonight?"

"That'd be great. See you then. I love you."

"I love you, too."

I hung up, relieved we'd made up but frustrated he still couldn't see that the girl was trying to cause trouble between us. However, we had more important things to think about. I wondered what Benjamin would think about the papers Laura had found in the safe-deposit box. And hid from me.

Ↄ

I tried to smile at the young girl slouched against the kitchen door, observing me with narrowed hazel eyes. Her cap sat backward on her head, with short lanks of ash-blond hair sticking out wildly around the edges.

"Sarah, stand up straight and say hello to Miz Storm." Mabel placed an arm around the girl's shoulders encouragingly.

Her granddaughter straightened, her eyes still boring into mine.

I licked my lips. What? Now I was going to let a ten-year-old intimidate me? A short one, at that.

"It's very nice to meet you, Sarah." I hoped I sounded grown-up, but had a feeling I wasn't fooling her a bit. "You can call me Victoria."

A spark of something flashed in her eyes, but then she

shrugged her shoulders, which looked solid in spite of her lean frame. "Okay."

What did I say next? I'd had very little contact with children, except for the Hansen monsters. And I held hopes they weren't typical.

School. That was it. "So what do you think of your new school?"

She sneered. "It stinks."

"Oh."

"Sarah Jane Carey." Mabel stood, hands on hips, her face red. "Is that any way to talk? Cedar Chapel Elementary is a very nice school."

Another shrug. I decided it was time to change the subject. Okay, how about food?

"I'll bet you're hungry, Sarah. How about some milk and cookies?"

"Okay." She flopped down on a kitchen chair and drummed her fingers against the table.

Mabel shook her head and placed three cookies on a plate then poured a glass of milk.

Okay, the food was a good idea. What next? Buster!

"Would you like to go with me to take Buster for a walk after you eat?"

"Who's Buster?" She crammed half a cookie into her mouth then followed it with a couple of gulps of milk. I hoped she'd chewed, but if so, I hadn't noticed.

"My dog."

"What dog?" She glanced around. "I don't see a dog. Don't hear one either. Don't even smell one."

Her eyes challenged me to produce the dog that wasn't there.

"He's in the backyard. I'll take you to meet him when you're finished eating."

The first glimmer of interest sparked in her eyes, and I breathed a sigh of relief. Maybe I'd found common ground after all.

I was glad the seniors were in their rooms resting now, except Martin, who was probably dozing in front of the TV. I was a little nervous about how they might react to the child. But they'd probably win her over in ten seconds flat. They'd won me over when I was younger than her. Nostalgia washed over me, and I swallowed. Mabel kept one eye on her granddaughter while she prepared a salad to go with the beef and noodles.

Sarah pushed her chair back, the legs scraping against the tiles. "Okay, let's go see that dog." Ignoring her napkin, she swiped the back of her hand across her mouth, then wiped it across the leg of her jeans.

Mabel gave me a grateful smile as I followed Sarah out the kitchen door. I opened the gate to the chain link fence and preceded Sarah into the yard, not sure how Buster would react to her presence. He had a love/hate relationship with the neighbor children, and I didn't think he'd bite but didn't want to take any chances.

He was curled up beneath the big oak tree, but we'd barely made it inside the fence before he came bounding across the yard. He stopped short and began to sniff around Sarah's small frame. She giggled, the first happy sound she'd emitted since she'd arrived at the lodge.

The next thing I knew, Sarah and Buster were romping and rolling across the ground. His excited barks blended with her laughter. Apparently it was love at first sight.

After I'd watched for a while to make sure all was well, I went back inside the house. Mabel was looking out the window, a big smile on her face.

"That Buster is just what my baby girl needs." She wiped at her eye.

"She's going to be fine. I'm sure of it." I patted her on her shoulder.

I poured a cup of coffee and went back to finish work in my office. When I came out again, Mabel was removing her apron. The muted sounds of shouts and laughter reached my ears.

Mabel waved toward the window. "Sarah's met some friends, it seems. I'll probably have to drag her away. But I don't mind. She needs friends."

I went to the window and peered through. Oh no. All three Hansen kids were running around the yard, whooping and screeching like a mob of wild banshees. I sighed and lifted a silent prayer up to God. Now there were four to make my life miserable. Shame pinched at me. I knew the Hansens weren't bad children. They were just full of mischief. Maybe I needed to put forth more of an effort to be friendly with them. Especially with winter coming. They were experts at not only making snowballs, but throwing them, too. Of course, I'd gotten them back a few times, but somehow they always came out ahead.

Miss Jane came downstairs just as Mabel and Sarah were leaving. Sarah was grubby from rolling on the ground with Buster. I hoped the grass stains would come out. When introduced to Miss Jane, she stuck her hand out and behaved with perfect manners.

"Why, such an adorable little girl." Miss Jane prattled around the kitchen, helping me to make the last-minute preparations for dinner. "She's going to be a real blessing, isn't she?"

"Sure, a real blessing," I muttered, as I carried serving dishes into the dining room.

For the first time in hours, I remembered the papers Laura Baker had tried to hide from me, and a quiver of excitement ran through me. Why would she have tried to hide them if they weren't important? Could they hold a clue to the whereabouts of the elusive jewels? Or perhaps some other decades-old secrets?

CHAPTER ⫼ ⫼⫼ ELEVEN

So, he couldn't come to dinner because he forgot a meeting, huh? Seething, I placed the last serving bowl on the sideboard. This made the second time in less than two weeks this had happened, and suspicion raised its ugly head and roared at me. What if the "meeting" was a date with the seductive Christiana Baker?

I hated the feeling coursing through me. And I hated my suspicious nature. Benjamin had never given me a real reason to doubt his faithfulness. But every time I thought about those catty eyes devouring him and mocking me, anger toward the little temptress rose up again.

Miss Jane called the rest of the seniors to dinner.

"Something sure smells good." Martin held his head back and sniffed loudly, then grinned.

"Mabel made a new beef and noodle recipe she found," I said. I filled water glasses and placed them on the table.

"That woman was sent from God," Georgina declared.

"What? My cooking wasn't good enough for you?" Miss Jane pouted and glared at her friend.

"Oh, I didn't mean that, Jane. Of course your cooking is wonderful." Miss Georgina hastened to smooth the ruffled feathers. "But you needed a break, I'm sure. That's all I meant."

I suppressed a grin at the quick answer. Miss Jane didn't look too convinced as she filled her salad plate and dished up a small bowl of soup. The dishes wobbled a little as she carried them to the table, and I wondered, not for the first time, if I should change the buffet style of our meals. It worked all right for breakfast. But dinner had soup, salad, main course, and dessert. Most of the seniors were strong and dexterous. But they were getting older, and perhaps I needed to make things easier for them.

"I wonder if Aggie is having dinner." Miss Jane's statement, coming out of the blue, sent a shock through my entire body.

Miss Georgina gasped. "Oh, poor Aggie. I can't bear to think of what she could be going through."

"Now cut it out, you two." Martin took Georgina's hand, seeming not to care who saw. "Look, Aggie is more than likely playing a big joke on everyone. Or else, she's forgotten there are people who worry about her. It wouldn't be the first time she's gone off and not let anyone know."

Martin was right about that. Miss Aggie had gone to Jefferson City to see her brother a couple of times without bothering to tell anyone. And once, she flew to St. Louis on the spur of the moment to go shopping at her favorite dress boutique. I hoped—no, prayed—that was the case this time. But the fact of the abandoned car with the left-behind broken bracelet caused me concern. Not to mention the cell phone that Miss Aggie loved.

We finished our meal in miserable silence.

After dinner, Frank and Martin went to the rec room to watch a movie. The ladies all pitched in as usual to help clean up, then we went to the parlor. After a while the clicking of three sets of knitting needles lulled me to a near-sleep state. I shielded a yawn with the back of my hand.

"I saw that, Victoria," Miss Jane said, her eyes twinkling. "You really should learn to knit. It's good exercise for the fingers."

"Uh-huh. But I don't think. . ." The phone rang, cutting off my admission that I had no desire to learn to knit. "I'll get it."

I stepped into the foyer and picked up the phone. "Cedar Lodge."

"Hi, it's Corky. Dad just called. They cut their trip short and came back home because of Aunt Aggie."

"Have they heard from her?" I closed my eyes. *Please God, please God.*

"No. No word. But their house shows signs of having been broken into, although nothing is missing."

Confusion and fear swirled through my mind. "Do they have any leads at all?"

"No, but Dad believes it may have something to do with Aunt Aggie's disappearance."

"But what possible connection could it have? Unless Miss Aggie has been staying there?"

"I don't know why she'd need to break in. All she had to do was ask, and Father would have given her a key."

"Then, what. . . ?"

"I don't know. Dad said it was just a gut feeling." He

sighed. "I thought you should know."

We hung up, and I walked slowly back into the parlor.

I returned to my chair and curled my feet up beneath me. "Simon Pennington's house was broken into."

"Oh my." Miss Georgina dropped the scarf she was knitting onto her lap.

"Oh no, this proves Aggie was kidnapped." Fear covered Miss Jane's face. "They took her because she could get them into Simon's house."

I tried, unsuccessfully, to follow her reasoning. "Why would anyone want to get into Simon's house?"

"How should I know, Victoria? He's a Pennington, that's why."

There was no reason I could think of why anyone would want to break into Simon's house. Unless. . .hmm, Jack Riley had once gone there when Miss Aggie was visiting Simon. He'd asked her if he could examine the Pennington diamonds. He'd then asked about the rumored emeralds. But no one knew where the emeralds were or even if they still existed. Could Mr. Riley have seen something there that interested him? Enough to break in to find it? He did leave Cedar Chapel mighty fast.

I glanced from Miss Jane to Miss Georgina. "You know we've suspected Clyde and Forrest of being mixed up in illegal actions. Maybe involving the Pennington emeralds." I spoke slowly, attempting to gather my thoughts. "Could Jack Riley have been involved as well?"

They looked at each other, then both shook their heads.

"I don't believe he was around Cedar Chapel during that time." Miss Jane looked thoughtful. "But of course,

Forrest wasn't actually either, so who knows? They could have sneaked back to Pennington House at night. Anyone could have hidden out in the smuggling cave and tunnel."

A few months earlier, while investigating the murder of the man found in the secret tunnel at Pennington House, we'd found another tunnel which led to a cave in the side of a hill. Wooden tracks leading from a secret room to the cave and on down to the river indicated some sort of smuggling activity in the past. Probably during or shortly after World War II.

Was it possible Clyde's murder, Miss Aggie's disappearance, and Jack Riley's sudden departure were all somehow connected to these earlier criminal activities? I knew Miss Aggie was innocent of any wrongdoing. Or at least, I was pretty sure. If she knew more than she'd admitted about the secrets of Pennington House, she could be in danger. We had to find her. And soon.

At the shrill ring of the phone, all three of us started. I shook my head and went to answer.

"Hi, honey." At sound of Ben's voice, relief washed over me.

"Hi, Benjamin. Your meeting over?"

"Yeah, it didn't last as long as I'd expected. Okay if I come over?"

Was it ever? Maybe he could chase away whatever ghosts were pursuing me tonight.

"Of course. Have you eaten?"

"Yes, I grabbed a couple of burgers before the meeting. Could use some coffee though."

"Okay, I'll make some."

"I need to drop paperwork off at the office, so it may be fifteen minutes or so before I get there."

"Okay, coffee'll be ready by then."

I made the coffee, put the kettle on for tea, then went back to the parlor.

"Ben's coming over. I'm going to print out the lists I've made before he gets here."

I headed for my office. It was time to lay what I had on the table for everyone. I glanced over the document.

Clyde Foster: Victim of accident or murder?

Clues:
1. *Whatzit's frantic cries of "No, no, get out."*
2. *Fragment of paper with letters n-n-e-l.*
3. *Suspicion of Clyde's illegal activities.*
4. *A 1968 copy of the* Gazette *with the story of the horse theft. (Which didn't mention Clyde was a suspect.)*
5. *Another article that revealed that Clyde had been arrested for the horse theft. (According to Mrs. Miller, his lawyer managed to get him off.)*

I added the facts surrounding Miss Aggie's disappearance, including her knowledge that her nephew wasn't at home. I listed the abandoned car and the items found in it. Then I typed in the latest news about the break-in.

Possible Suspects:
1. *Laura Baker*

2. *Christiana Baker*
3. *Jack Riley*

Who had a motive to kill Clyde?
   1. His daughter, Laura:
      a. To get revenge for his treatment of her mother?
      b. Addition: Laura has found papers (perhaps letters?), which she tried to cover up, in Clyde's safe-deposit box. Why would she hide them from me?
      c. She has put the shop up for sale and indicated she needs money.
   2. Christiana: Motive unknown. Addition: same as c above.
   3. Someone who suspected he knew the location of the Pennington jewels?
   4. Someone who suspected he knew they were involved with the theft/disappearance of Pennington jewels?
   5. Jack Riley for the suspect in 3 and 4 (absolutely no clues, just a gut feeling).
   6. Or could it be possible that Mrs. Miller was right and Clyde had stolen Burly Anderson's prize horse? But Mr. Anderson was eighty-five, and his sons both lived in Chicago. Anyway, forty years was a long time to hold a grudge strong enough to kill for. (Mrs. Miller claims to have seen Gabe, the younger son, in town the night before Clyde's murder.)

I printed the document and carried it to the parlor with me. Benjamin arrived a few minutes later. He helped me bring in the tea cart, then went to the rec room and asked Frank and Martin to join us. I'd placed a few cookies on a plate as well.

After everyone had their drinks and sweets, I handed the list to Benjamin and asked him to pass it around. Finally, Martin handed it to me.

"What are your thoughts about it?" I asked.

"Corky's going to be awfully mad at you if he sees this." Martin shook his head.

The same thing had crossed my mind, which was one reason I hadn't asked him and Phoebe to be here. "I know, but Jack Riley is a possible suspect."

"I can't really see that, Victoria." Ben frowned. "You've suspected him of things before, and he always turned out to be innocent."

"He could be innocent of certain things and guilty of something bigger. It seems obvious to me he knows something. I believe he's always known something. I'm just not sure what yet."

"Who is Christiana?" Frank asked. "You haven't written anything by her name, but you have her on here twice."

"Yeah," Benjamin muttered. "I noticed that, too."

Heat burned my face, but I pressed my lips together and lifted my chin. "She's Laura Baker's daughter, Frank. It's just a hunch, but I'm pretty sure she knows something."

Benjamin gave me a side grin, which made me want to punch him. He probably still thought I was jealous. I narrowed my eyes. He'd better not say it.

He winked. "Okay, let's talk about this horse theft thing."

"Mrs. Miller told me about it first. She's convinced Clyde stole the horse, and I did see an old *Gazette* article about him being arrested for it. But he wasn't convicted."

"And Janis saw Gabe in town the night before Clyde's death?" Miss Evalina had been silent until now.

"Yes, ma'am. Of course that doesn't necessarily mean anything. He could have been visiting one of his cousins who live around the area."

"It does place him here," Frank said. "But I doubt he'd have killed Clyde over a suspected horse theft. Especially that many years ago."

"They used to string up horse thieves," Martin said with undisguised relish. "But they didn't wait forty years to do it. They took them to the closest tree and—"

"Martin!" Miss Georgina's voice sounded horrified, and I didn't blame her.

"We get the idea, Martin." Miss Evalina gave him a pointed look.

"Sorry."

Frank glanced at Benjamin. "What do you think, Ben? Does any of it make sense?"

"I'm not sure." He gave a little laugh. "Victoria, you seem to have a lot of suspects with very little evidence."

"I know that," I said. "I simply jotted down some ideas and observations with a few clues thrown in. That's why I wanted input from the rest of you."

"So, Clyde's daughter is selling the shop," Miss Georgina said. "I wonder where the animals will go."

"I don't know. I suggested she announce the sale to pet-store owners in the area."

"Aggie might want Whatzit," Martin said.

"He might make a colorful mascot for the new hotel," I said.

Chuckles broke out, then stopped. We all glanced around with stricken looks. My heart felt like a stone. Where was she? And more important, was she alive and well?

C03

Benjamin tossed a small log on the fire and sat beside me on the love seat. The seniors had gone to bed, and we'd sat mostly in silence for the last hour, cuddled up in front of the fireplace.

"Do you think we should postpone the wedding?" I'd dreaded bringing up the subject, but we had to talk about it.

Benjamin groaned. "No, please, honey."

"But we can't get married with Miss Aggie missing. I couldn't bear it."

He rubbed my shoulder and sighed. "I know. But let's not make that decision yet. Miss Aggie could turn up any day. In fact, I expect her to."

A spark of hope flared inside me at his words. "Do you really? Do you think she might be okay?"

"Yes, I do." He leaned over and kissed the top of my head. "And so does Corky."

"He does?"

"Yeah. His take on it is that she left the car behind on purpose, so she couldn't be traced and then rented another car."

"But why would she do that?"

"Corky says she's been afraid of something since Clyde's death. He thinks she ran away to hide."

"But why wouldn't she tell us so we wouldn't worry?"

"Because the more people who know, the more chance the murderer could find her. At least, that's what Corky believes is going on in her mind, and I'm inclined to agree with him."

"Oh, I hope you're both right. I don't know what we'll do if something has happened to Miss Aggie. Nothing will ever be the same."

"Now, sweetheart, don't talk like that. You can't give up hope." He traced my cheek with his thumb, and I leaned back against his arm and looked at him through half-closed eyes.

He pulled me closer and leaned toward me.

A sudden thought struck. "Ben!" I sat up straight, and he yipped like a puppy.

"Vickie, you hit me right in the mouth with your head."

"Oh, I'm so sorry. But I just had a thought. What if Miss Aggie is holed up somewhere at Pennington House?"

He sighed and rubbed his lip, which looked like it might be swelling.

"Does it hurt?" Guilt riddled me, and I reached toward his puffy lip.

He jerked his head back as though I was going to sock him. The big baby.

"Not much. It's okay. But to get back to your question, Miss Aggie is not at Pennington House."

"How do you know? We need to search and make sure."

"Corky thought of it from the beginning. He scoured every inch of the place, including the tunnels and the cave." He shook his head. "She's not there, Vickie."

"Okay." But I wasn't convinced. I wouldn't be satisfied she wasn't there until I had checked the house and property myself. With some help from the seniors, of course.

"Don't even think about it." Benjamin turned a stern look

on me. "I know that look in your eyes, Victoria."

I couldn't help the breath of exasperation that escaped from my throat. He knew me too well. "I don't know why you always get the idea I'm up to something. Because I'm not." Well, nothing I'd planned out anyway.

"Umm-hmm." He stood. "I'd better go. It's getting late. But if you absolutely must search Pennington House, ask Corky first. Don't be sneaking around."

I frowned at him as I walked beside him to the door, his arm still around me. He chuckled and leaned down to kiss me, then apparently thought better of it. He gave me a quick hug instead, said good night, and left.

I locked the door and headed upstairs, the idea that had germinated in my brain now growing tendrils. Corky would let me search, but he'd want to lead the way—and if he'd already searched and found nothing, that wouldn't help at all. But when the workers left for the weekend, Corky would more than likely go to Jefferson City to see his parents.

I brushed my teeth and got into my pajamas, then crawled between the cool sheets and pulled my comforter up to my chin. I'd better run my current plan before God and see what He thought. Of course, I was pretty sure He wouldn't condone me sneaking into Pennington House, so maybe I'd better get permission after all. I'd wait until Corky was ready to leave town, so he wouldn't insist on escorting me through the place. My last thought before I dropped off to sleep was directed toward God.

Lord, please keep me on the straight and narrow and control my willfulness.

CHAPTER TWELVE

It was nine in the morning, so the truck stop parking lot only had a scattering of vehicles. I spied Phoebe's Altima parked near the building and pulled the van into the space beside it, battling a smidgen of envy as my eyes glanced off the shiny, apple-red coupe.

For the jillionth time, I wondered if I could afford the payments on a new car. But even though the lodge was doing well, I'd resolved to keep most of the income, as well as my inheritance, in the bank for emergency repairs and other things.

For the first time, I considered taking Dad up on his offer of a new car. But the thought passed, and I shook my head at my moment of weakness. I was independent and planned on staying that way.

A country song was playing as I walked into the restaurant. I spotted Phoebe and headed for her booth.

"Isn't this cool?" Her eyes danced with excitement. "This is the first time I've been here."

"Yes, it is nice." I slipped into the seat across from her and ran my hand over the shining table top. "I love the newness of the place."

"Me, too. It even smells new."

"It also smells like breakfast, which I skipped this morning." My stomach rumbled in agreement.

"Well, that's the point of meeting for breakfast, silly." She giggled, and I grinned in response. Phoebe and I were almost exact opposites in personality. Nevertheless, we'd formed a deep friendship. "I'm so glad we have these second Saturday breakfasts together, aren't you?"

"Absolutely. And our monthly lunches." Of course Phoebe and I saw each other at the lodge, and sometimes we made a foursome with Corky and Benjamin to go to a movie or out to dinner. But our girls-only meetings were special and had helped us get to know each other better.

"None of the staff here are locals," she whispered. "Or at least I don't know any of them."

I glanced around. She seemed to be right. "They probably drive over from Branson or Caffee Springs."

"If any of them are from Branson, I feel sorry for them when the ice and snow hit." She nodded emphatically, then smiled at the waitress who stopped at our booth, menus in hand.

"Would you like something to drink?" Her smile was friendly as she laid the menus on the table.

"I'll have a Coke." Phoebe flashed her a grin. "And I'd like pancakes and sausage please. Two of each."

Good grief. Coke with pancakes?

"Coffee, please, and a glass of water." I glanced over the menu, then placed an order for bacon and scrambled eggs with wheat toast.

When the waitress left, Phoebe looked at me and shook her head. "Why do you bother to look at a menu? You know you always order the same thing."

"Not always."

"When did you not?" she challenged.

"Hmm. Let's see. Oh, never mind." I laughed at her satisfied grin.

Our food came, and we bowed our heads and prayed silently, then dug in.

"Why, that's Uncle Jack." Phoebe's voice held surprise as well as excitement. "I wonder when he got back."

I turned my head slightly. Sure enough, Jack Riley had entered. I caught my breath as the sheriff followed him in. They found a booth across the room from us.

"Now why would he be with the sheriff?" I mused aloud.

"Why? What do you mean?" Phoebe frowned, and I realized I'd done it again.

"Uh, nothing. I just didn't know they were friends."

"Oh." Her face relaxed. "I thought you were making another of your cracks about Uncle Jack."

"No. Of course not." But I couldn't help wonder if perhaps the sheriff was suspicious of the man. Maybe he was investigating him. But on the sly. Of course, subtlety wasn't Bob Turner's usual tactic. I couldn't really see him asking someone to breakfast to investigate them.

"Phoebe, would you like to ask them to join us? I know it's been over a week since you've seen your uncle."

"What a great idea. Thanks, I think I will." She jumped up and headed across the room. Both men looked up in surprise when she appeared at their booth. Her uncle smiled and started to scoot over, but she shook her head. I couldn't hear what they were saying, but a few moments later, she came back and sat down.

"Are they joining us?"

"No. They're talking business, but Uncle Jack will be at my house by dinnertime. He just got back this morning."

My ears perked up. "Back from where?"

She shrugged and took a bite of pancake, following it with a drink from her Coke glass. I shuddered.

"You don't know?" I should probably drop the subject, but how would I ever find out anything if I didn't ask questions? Phoebe certainly wasn't volunteering information. Of course, she didn't know how badly I wanted to know, and I couldn't tell her.

"He didn't say. What difference does it make?" She darted a suspicious glance at me, and I knew it was time to change the subject.

"Oh, I just wondered. I thought maybe he'd have another adventure to tell us about."

"Well, my goodness, Victoria. He doesn't just go from one adventure to another. He has business to take care of, too, you know."

I nodded. "So when do you go for your fitting?"

Her eyes lit up. "Next Tuesday. I'm hoping you'll go with me. Mother can't get off work."

"I'd love to. What time?" I meant it, too. I couldn't wait to see Phoebe in her wedding dress. I'd be having mine fitted in a couple of weeks.

"Two o'clock. But I thought if you wanted we could leave

REST IN PEACE 143

early and have lunch in Springfield."

"Okay, but I'm not going to that place that throws your rolls at you."

She laughed. She, Corky, and Benjamin had been trying to get me to that restaurant for months, claiming the homestyle food was great and the atmosphere fun, but I wasn't buying it. After all, how much fun could it be to have food thrown at you?

 C3

I bolted upright in bed, blinking in the sudden light, my heart hammering. The phone on my bedside table rang again. I grabbed the receiver. "Cedar Lodge."

"Victoria? Were you asleep?" Corky's voice held surprise and something else.

I glanced at the clock. The display flashed 10:30. "Yeah, I must have dropped off to sleep while I was reading. What's wrong?"

He didn't say anything. "Corky?"

"My father just called. They found Aunt Aggie's suitcase in a Dumpster behind the bus station."

A chill slithered down my spine. I sat bolt upright, my heart hammering against my ribs. "What?"

"Someone found Aunt Aggie's suitcase in a Dumpster behind the Jefferson City Bus Station," he repeated. I heard him take a deep breath. "There were traces of blood on some of the items inside."

I gasped and tried to breathe normally. "Oh no. Oh Corky, no. Dear God."

"I'm going to call Benjamin, and we'll probably come over if that's all right."

"Yes, please do. Please get here as soon as you can."

I yanked on a pair of jeans and a sweatshirt, then crammed my feet into a pair of moccasins. I bolted down the first flight of stairs, taking the steps two at a time, then slowed down and tried to be quiet as I walked down the second floor hallway to the next flight of stairs. I couldn't face the seniors with this news. Not by myself.

I started the coffeemaker and got a fire going in the parlor. Horrible pictures invaded my mind. What-ifs pounded me mercilessly.

I piled cups and saucers, spoons, sugar, and cream on a tray, and set it on the counter by the coffeemaker.

The doorbell rang, and I hurried to let them in. Benjamin stood there alone. He took one look at my face and pulled me into his arms.

The sobs broke loose. Sobs I'd been holding back since Corky's phone call.

"It's okay, honey. Let it out." Benjamin's voice and the gentle caressing on my back soothed me, and finally the wracking sobs dwindled to an occasional whimper. After one more gentle pat, he lifted my chin and searched my face, then gave me a kiss on the forehead.

"Thanks, I'm okay." I tried to smile but felt my lips tremble with the effort.

Through the open door, I saw Corky's truck pull up. He jumped out, went around and opened the passenger door, and Phoebe stepped down.

I went to the kitchen and filled a thermal decanter with coffee, then took the tray to the parlor.

The four of us sat in stunned silence, casting somber

glances at each other as we drank the hot coffee.

Benjamin set his cup on the tray and cleared his throat. "Corky, could you tell us again, just what your father said?"

Corky inhaled deeply, then let the air out in a rush. "This afternoon Dad received a call from the police department. They said they'd found something that might belong to Aunt Aggie and asked him to come downtown and take a look. When he arrived at the station, they showed him a suitcase. He was pretty sure it was Aunt Aggie's. Then they said the tag on the luggage had her name and the Cedar Lodge address.

"Finally, they opened the case and let him view the contents. He recognized some of the clothing right away. And he identified the silver hairbrush and mirror. Then they told him the maintenance man found the suitcase in the Dumpster behind the bus station. By that time, Dad was worried sick, wondering why the bag was in the Dumpster, but there was more. They told him they found traces of blood on one article of clothing. They'd send it to the lab, but they don't want to trust the hairbrush because someone else may have used it. They needed an uncontaminated article of her clothing or something she'd used. Dad took them some things from the house that belonged to her." His voice cracked on the last word, and Phoebe leaned closer to him and took his hand.

"So. . ." I tried to speak but could barely get a sound out past the lump. I swallowed and tried again. "When will they get the lab results?"

"Not sure. They told Dad they'd try to get a rush on it. It could take a day and a half or a month. They're checking fingerprints on the suitcase and contents, too. They got Aunt

Aggie's prints on a couple of things at Dad's. If they find anyone's besides hers, we'll all need to go to the sheriff's office and get printed so they can rule out our prints."

I closed my eyes tightly. How could we wait that long to find out if the blood was Miss Aggie's? And what if there were someone else's prints? Would that prove foul play?

"Vickie, are you going to tell the seniors?" At the sound of Benjamin's voice, I opened my eyes.

The seniors? How could I tell them such horrible news? But if I didn't, what if someone else told them?

"Does anyone else know?" I asked.

"No, just Dad and the four of us. Oh, and Sheriff Turner. The police called him to let him know they had a lead."

"Let's wait until they get the test results before we say anything. Maybe someone stole her suitcase, and when they didn't find any money or jewelry, they stuffed it in the trash. Maybe it's not even her blood."

"You're right. They're all worried enough as it is. There's no sense in putting this on them until we know more."

"Put what on us?" Miss Evalina stood in the doorway with Frank right behind her.

ભ

I woke up the next morning with a horrible headache. After we'd told Miss Evalina and Frank the details, they'd agreed to wait until we had more information to tell the rest of the seniors. Then, with sick expressions on their faces, they'd walked slowly upstairs to their suite.

Sleep had come to me in sporadic ten-minute doses throughout the night. The next morning I went downstairs on wobbly legs. Miss Jane was already in the kitchen, and the aroma of frying bacon and sausage greeted me.

"Good, you're finally here." Miss Jane tossed me a playful scowl to let me know she was kidding. "You can scramble the eggs while I finish the pancakes."

I was happy to see she was too distracted with her preparations to notice anything amiss with me.

I did as I was told, and breakfast was soon done and placed in serving dishes on the sideboard next to pitchers of orange and apple juice.

I went back to the kitchen for the toast caddies, and while I was there, I heard the seniors entering the dining room. I had to get myself together before I faced them, so I stayed where I was for a moment, listening to the familiar voices that floated through the door. Then I put on a pleasant expression and walked in.

I was greeted with their usual banter and replied with what I hoped was my normal manner. Sunday breakfast was usually rushed, and today was no different. They got up one by one to go finish getting ready for church. As Miss Evalina passed my chair on her way out, she placed her hand on my shoulder for just a moment. I reached up and touched her hand briefly, glad to be able to share a moment of sympathy with someone who understood.

After I'd cleared away the breakfast things and turned on the filled dishwasher, I went up to shower and get ready for my own church service. For once I was glad we all attended different churches.

Benjamin picked me up, and we drove to church together. We entered the sanctuary of Cedar Chapel Community Church and found a seat near the front. The worship team took their places a few minutes later, and the band began to play. Between my headache and the worry, I had trouble entering in to the worship at first. But finally, peace penetrated my heart and soul, and I slowly began to relax.

Pastor Carl's message was about the Holy Spirit as Comforter. Benjamin squeezed my hand, and I squeezed back to tell him I understood. I sent a prayer of thanks up to my heavenly Father for the timely word. And by the time the service was over, I'd done my best to leave Miss Aggie in the Lord's hands.

Frank and Miss Evalina were going to his son's house for the afternoon, and Martin was also spending the day with his family. Benjamin ate dinner with Miss Jane, Miss Georgina, and me. Afterwards, the ladies went to the rec room and played dominoes most of the afternoon. I hardly saw them at all except at suppertime.

Ben didn't stay long, as he still had to get the *Gazette* ready for the next day's issue. I walked out on the porch with him.

"Honey, try not to worry. I'll be over in the morning as soon as I can, and we'll wait for Corky's call together." He kissed me good-bye then waited until I was inside with the door locked before he left.

Try not to worry? How could I keep from it?

Restless, I went upstairs, planning to go to my suite. I stopped at Miss Aggie's door. I stood there for a moment with my hand on the knob, then turned it and went in.

The aroma of Chanel No. 5 assailed my nostrils. Miss Aggie's scent. Tears welled up. I'd never been as close to Miss Aggie as some of the others, but I cared about her deeply.

The very thought that she might be injured or even dead was too much to bear.

I glanced around the neat room. A trace of powder on her dresser was the only thing that marred the tidiness. I grabbed a tissue from the box on her nightstand and wiped it across the dresser top.

"Where are you, Miss Aggie?" I whispered.

I walked over to the chest of drawers and looked at the black-and-white photo that stood in an antique frame.

Four young girls in their midteens stood with arms linked on the lawn in front of Pennington House. Miss Aggie, Miss Jane, Miss Georgina, and Miss Evalina. Laughter was on each face that held innocence rarely found these days. I knew their friendship was shattered for a while, but after all these years the four were still best friends. I sighed and went back downstairs. No sense in going to my apartment. I wouldn't be able to relax anyway.

Martin got home around seven and flopped onto the sofa in the rec room to watch a movie. When I peeked in a little later, Miss Georgina put her finger to her lips and motioned to the sofa. Martin had fallen asleep. I smiled and nodded and went to the parlor, curling up in an overstuffed chair with a book by one of my favorite authors.

By eight, Frank and Miss Evalina were home. She took one look at my face, walked over to me and put her arms around me, giving me a slight hug. Then she and Frank went upstairs.

After everyone was settled for the night, I went up to my own apartment. I changed into my pajamas and went to bed, thanking God for getting me through the day without having to tell the seniors about Miss Aggie's suitcase and the traces of blood that might be hers.

ᘓ

The clock was getting on my nerves. Each strike knifed through my brain. By the time it finally reached ten, I was ready to throw it in the fireplace. The peace I'd experienced in church on Sunday hadn't lasted long. This, I decided, was proof my faith wasn't as strong as it ought to be. Now, a week later, we'd finally gotten word that the DNA results were back.

I caught Benjamin's eye as I paced the floor. How could he sit there so calmly? I knew he was on edge, but you'd never know it by his demeanor. Corky had promised to phone us as soon as his father called him with the results of the DNA test.

Mabel had stuck her head in the door a few minutes before and asked if we needed anything. She'd picked up on something, probably because I'd totally lost control and burst into tears after the seniors had left for the center. I'd asked her to bring coffee for Benjamin, and she'd brought in a tray a few minutes later. She threw me a worried, questioning look, but I turned away, pretending not to notice. She shook her head and returned to the kitchen.

"Sweetheart, why don't you sit with me here on the sofa? You're going to be exhausted from pacing the floor."

"I can't sit. . . ."

Benjamin's cell phone rang, and I hurried over and sat by him as he answered. "Grant here."

He listened and shook his head to let me know it wasn't Corky. I sighed and jumped up. Pacing the floor was easier than sitting still with a million thoughts running through my head. Ben snapped his phone closed, and it rang again almost immediately. I held my breath and stared as he answered. He listened, then closed his eyes.

"Ben, what is it? Is that Corky?" I sat beside him again.

"Okay. Sorry, Corky. We'll be praying."

He looked at me and pulled me close. "Honey, the blood on the clothing was Miss Aggie's."

CHAPTER THIRTEEN

I waved a limp hand as Benjamin drove away. He and Corky were heading out to Jefferson City in a couple of hours. Benjamin had friends on the police force there as well as on the staff of the *News Tribune*. There was a possibility he could obtain news and information about the case that wouldn't be available yet to the family.

I shut the door and stepped into the great hall. Standing in the doorway, I looked up at Franklin Storm's portrait. Family—and town rumor—had it that my ancestor had indentured himself to obtain boat passage to the shores of this country, one of the few ways in those days to avoid debtors' prison. Whatever the truth was, Franklin Storm cleared the way in this area for others looking for a home and freedom. He must have been a strong man with a goal for the future and determination to achieve it.

If only I could tap into that strength. I sank into a chair and leaned back, letting the tears flow. How could I tell these precious senior friends that their childhood and life-long friend had more than likely met with disaster? Or at the least, injury. But possibly even murder.

I needed that Storm family strength now. I raised my eyes

once more to the portrait, and my gaze fell on the black book he held clutched near his heart. I inhaled sharply, the breath permeating my lungs. A thrill ran through me. I did have that strength. Only it wasn't Storm family strength. It was the strength of the Holy Spirit, promised and bequeathed by my Savior, Jesus Christ.

The seniors had that strength as well. I breathed a silent prayer of thanks and went to the kitchen to put water on for tea. We would need it.

Mabel was frosting an oatmeal cake, and the homey aroma soothed me as I entered the kitchen. I filled the kettle and put it on the burner. "Mabel, when the seniors arrive ,would you please join us in the parlor? I have some news and need to talk about it before Sarah gets off the school bus."

"Yes ma'am. I'll bring the tea in."

"Thanks. And maybe a pitcher of ice water."

It would be an hour or so before they got home from the center. I checked to make sure there was wood in the container by the corner fireplace, and as an added measure, I pulled a few knitted afghans from the wicker trunk in the opposite corner.

I sat in an easy chair and closed my eyes to pray. The ring of the doorbell jerked me awake. I heard Mabel's footsteps padding to the door, so I stayed where I was.

"Miss Storm, I wonder if I might speak to you for a moment." Surprised, I stared into Laura Baker's shadowed eyes.

"Of course. Won't you come in?" I indicated a chair near my own with a small table between.

Laura shook her head, fidgeting with a manila envelope she held. Her eyes darted around the room. "I don't have time to stay. I must return home to take care of business there."

"Is Christiana going with you?" I sincerely hoped so.

"No, she insists on staying behind in case we get a buyer for the pet store. She'll have to stay in the apartment. The hotel expenses are simply too much for me just now."

Suddenly she held the envelope out to me, her hand shaking. "I'd like for you to have these. I'll need them back eventually, but I don't have time to deal with them now."

"Are they important?" As I took the envelope, a shiver ran up my arm. This was way too easy.

"I have no idea. Most of the documents are in German, and as I said, I don't have time to deal with them. "

"In German? Are you sure?"

"My father's mother was German. I understand he spoke the language fairly well. And apparently read it as well." She narrowed her eyes. "They are more than likely simply personal letters and business documents. If you do manage to get them translated, I would appreciate you making copies and sending me the originals."

"Certainly. I'll be more than happy to do that. But what if. . .what if they should pertain in some way to Clyde's death or some other crime?"

"That's what I'm afraid of, Miss Storm." Her voice was barely above a whisper. She ran her tongue over her lips and took a deep breath.

What was she afraid of? Did she think whoever had killed her father might come after her, too?

"Laura, why are you so afraid?"

"Why?" A nervous laugh burst from her lips. "I want the truth to come out. I don't know what my dad was mixed up in, but I fear for my daughter's safety. . .and my own. In case you do find something pertinent, of course you will need to give them to the authorities."

"Of course. . .but why me? You barely know me."

She searched my face for a moment. I wasn't sure what she was looking for. She shuddered. The woman seemed almost frightened out of her wits.

"I've heard about the other recent crimes and that you played a major role in solving them. I thought, perhaps. . ." She blinked, and the look she gave me was pleading. "Will you do this for me or not?"

"Very well. I'll do everything I can to get these translated. You have my word."

She nodded and offered her hand. "Thank you, Miss Storm."

"If we're going to be friends, Laura, you really must stop addressing me formally."

She nodded again, briefly. "Very well. Good-bye then, Victoria."

I watched from the front door as she drove away, and a moment of pity and regret struck me. It would have been nice if we could have truly been friends.

I returned to the parlor and glanced at the clock. The seniors would be arriving any minute, so there was no time to look through the envelope. I hurried to my office and locked the papers in the safe. The seniors would need my full attention.

Pains in my stomach reminded me I'd nibbled at breakfast and skipped lunch entirely. I went to the kitchen.

Mabel glanced up from the tea cart she was preparing. Little doilies, dainty cups and saucers, a plate of tiny sandwiches and another of shortbread. She motioned to the table.

"I thought you might be ready to eat a bite before the gang gets here." A sandwich cut diagonally rested on a small plate with a glass of milk beside it. Tears sprang into my eyes.

"Thank you, Mabel," I whispered. Sometimes I thought she could read my mind.

I'd finished my late lunch and put the dishes in the dishwasher when the seniors arrived home.

They usually came in happy but tired from the center. Today was no different. Their smiles were more than a match for their obvious weariness.

I thought briefly of waiting until later to tell them the news, but I knew I couldn't put it off.

The three ladies came in through the kitchen. I hoped Frank and Martin hadn't gone on one of their flea market sprees. Relieved, I heard Martin's laughter, and both men came through the door.

"Victoria, you won't believe who came to the center today." Miss Jane's eyes were bright with humor.

"Oh? And who would that be?"

"Janis, of all people." Miss Georgina giggled. "She's always thought she was above the goings-on, as she called them, at the center."

"Now, don't be unkind," Miss Evalina said. "I'm happy she finally decided to join us."

"I am, too." Miss Georgina darted a shamed look at her cousin. "And after the first little while, she seemed to enjoy herself. Didn't you think so, Jane?"

"I guess." She glanced around. "What's the tea cart for?"

I swallowed past the sudden lump in my throat. "I need to talk to everyone." I motioned toward the parlor door.

Each face froze with an expression of dread. Oh Lord, how could I possibly do this?

Frank took charge. "Okay, let's go to the parlor. Stop looking like somebody die—" He stopped and peered in my face, then put a protective arm around Miss Evalina. He guided her to the parlor, and the others followed. I motioned for Mabel to take the cart in, then followed her.

Everyone settled onto chairs and sofas while Mabel poured and handed out cups of tea. She gave me mine last.

"Mabel, please sit down." She sat on a wing chair, and I remained standing in the middle of the room, taking in every precious face.

"Aggie's dead, isn't she?" Miss Jane's face crumpled. She and Miss Aggie had been girlhood best friends, and there was still a special bond between them.

Gasps and little moans seemed to emit from every inch of the room, as though the room itself were mourning.

"Wait." I held my hand up, and five hopeful faces looked at me.

"We don't know." I glanced around at the hope mixed with fear on each face and knew I had to get it over with. "Miss Aggie's suitcase was discovered in a Dumpster behind the Jefferson City bus station. It was full of clothing and personal items. One article of clothing had traces of blood."

"Aggie's?" Miss Jane murmured.

"Yes, I'm afraid so." At the cries that burst forth, I once more held my hand up. "Please. They have no evidence that Miss Aggie is dead. Someone may have stolen the suitcase."

"But the blood!" Martin cried. "How could Miz Brown's blood get in the suitcase if someone else had it?"

"I don't know, Martin. Benjamin and Corky are in Jefferson City now trying to get more information. They'll call if they have anything. In the meantime, we need to think positive and hope and pray for the best."

"Victoria is right. And the first thing we need to do is pray." Miss Evalina bowed her head, and we followed suit. Then she led us in a heartfelt prayer that Miss Aggie would be found alive and well.

∓

The seniors remained in the parlor all afternoon, instead of splitting up as they customarily did. Neither Benjamin nor Corky had called, but I was pretty sure I'd hear from Benjamin before bedtime, if only to say good night. As I passed through the kitchen on my way to check out the small back parlor, I heard whispers and went in.

Sarah stood on tiptoe, whispering in her grandmother's ear. But her stage whisper wasn't very quiet. "Grandma, why do I have to be quiet?"

"You don't have to, Sarah," I said. A little noise might be just what the seniors need to get their minds off things. I smiled, and she gave me her usual "I don't care" look.

"I didn't want her bothering the old folks." Mabel reached over and tucked a strand of Sarah's unruly hair behind her ears. The little girl ducked and reached up to make sure her hat hadn't been upset.

"It's okay. Why don't you let her play?" I turned to Sarah. "Or maybe you'd like to go for a walk with Buster and me."

She darted a look at her grandmother, who gave her a nod and a smile.

"Can I hold his leash?"

"I don't see why not."

"Okay. I'll go." Wow. We seemed to be holding an actual conversation.

"Do we need coats? I haven't bothered to check the weather. I've been inside all day."

"Naw." Sarah waved her hand. "It's not cold. Are you ready to go now?"

"Sure, do you want to get the leash?"

She ran over and slipped Buster's leash off the hook by the door. "Bye Grandma. See you later."

"Okay baby, you mind Miz Storm."

"I will. I promise." She ran out the back door and into the fenced yard, where Buster greeted her with excited, ear-splitting barks.

"Do you know how to clip it on his collar?"

She frowned and threw me a look of disdain. "Of course. What do you think I am, a stupid baby or something?"

And we'd been doing so well. Or so I'd thought. "Sorry. I didn't mean that at all."

"Okay. Then I'm sorry, too." She leaned over, and Buster licked her face as she hooked the leash onto his collar. Giggling, she wiped her hand across her face. "Okay Buster boy, let's go."

When we got to the sidewalk, she stopped and looked at

me with a question in her eyes. "Which way?"

"You choose." It didn't really matter. Mrs. Miller was probably resting from her day at the center.

"Hey, Sarah!" The Hansen children came running across the street. "Where you going?"

"Taking Buster for a walk." She reached down and patted Buster on the head, and the other children followed suit. He didn't growl or bark, so apparently they'd made friends with him.

Sarah and Buster headed down the sidewalk, the dog practically dragging her, which didn't seem to bother her a bit. She just picked up her pace, flanked by the Hansen children.

"Don't go too fast now," I called after them. Too late. Mrs. Miller's cat streaked across the street, and Buster lit after it with the four children tearing behind, cheering him on.

"Look both ways before you cross that street again!" I yelled. But Buster and his gang of followers had disappeared around the corner.

I stopped in my tracks, berating myself for being so ignorant of children. I should have known better.

Someone guffawed loudly behind me. I whirled to see Mrs. Miller coming across the yard. "I see he got away from you again. You're not very good with animals, are you?"

Indignant, I opened my mouth, then, thinking better of it, shut it again. I took a deep breath. "Actually, I never had him in the first place. Someone else was holding his leash."

"Yes, I noticed. You don't know too much about children either, do you?"

I bit my lip and mentally counted to ten. "No, Mrs. Miller,

I don't." I started to head off after the children.

"You might as well wait for them here. As soon as Buster sees he's lost Fluffy, he'll head back this way looking for you."

"You may be right, but I think I'd better go look for them."

I got halfway down the block when I heard barking and laughing from somewhere behind me. Buster came galloping around the corner with all four children skipping around him. How did Mrs. Miller always know everything?

They ran up to me with grinning faces, including Buster's. His tongue was also hanging out.

"Looks like you all had fun." Who could keep from laughing along with those cheery faces?

"Yeah," they chorused.

"Did Buster do his business?"

"Nope, he just chased the cat till it ran up a tree." The youngest boy grinned. "It just sat up there on that ole branch, spitting at Buster. Boy, was he mad."

"Can we take him around again?" Sarah pleaded.

I sighed. Why not? No harm done that I could see.

"Okay, but I'm going with you this time, and Sarah, be sure to hang on to him. Especially if you see a cat."

We paraded around the block and arrived back at the lodge, mission accomplished and no mishaps.

The Hansens, whose names I now knew were Bobby, Charlie, and Cindy, waved and ran home. I went inside and let Sarah take care of Buster. She came in a few minutes later and hung the leash on its hook.

"Thanks for the help." I smiled at Sarah, hoping to get one back.

She shrugged. "Welcome."

She and Mabel left a few minutes later, and I went to wash up. When I got back down to the kitchen, Miss Jane was getting things together to take to the sideboard.

Dinner was quieter than usual. When we'd finished, Miss Evalina asked us all if we could meet in the parlor again.

I supposed she wanted to be with everyone. And that was fine with me. I didn't want to be alone with my thoughts either.

I told them I'd join them as soon as I'd finished cleaning up. But the ladies all pitched in, and within fifteen minutes we were finished and gathered together in the parlor. Flames leaped and logs crackled in the fireplace.

Silence hung heavily in the room, and faces were long and drawn.

"All right, we need to snap out of it." Miss Evalina's voice was kind but firm. "I didn't ask everyone to meet so we could sit around depressed and gloomy."

"I don't know why we're in here at all." Martin's voice broke. "I'd just as soon go watch a movie and get my mind off everything."

Miss Evalina shook her head. "No, we have to decide what to do."

"What?" Miss Jane's voice held surprise. "What can we do? Pray they find Aggie's body so we can give her a proper funeral and burial?"

"Stop it, Jane." For the first time, Miss Evalina spoke sharply. "Let's not bury her until we know she's really dead. I, for one, don't believe it for a minute."

Miss Jane sat up straight, hope in her eyes. "You don't? Really, Eva?"

"No. Aggie's too smart to get herself killed. And we all seem to forget the mysterious circumstances of her leaving."

We looked around at each other.

"Dang. She's right." Martin smacked himself on the leg and chortled. "This is all just a big cover-up for whatever it is she's up to."

Oh, how I hoped they were right. But even if the sheriff was right about the clasp breaking on Miss Aggie's pearls, the suitcase in the Dumpster made me worry. And, of course, Miss Aggie's blood. But I wasn't going to voice my fears.

"I think all the answers to Clyde's death and Aggie's disappearance are right here in Cedar Chapel."

"But Eva, we searched Clyde's shop. There was nothing there."

I hit myself on the forehead with the palm of my hand. "Oh my goodness. I almost forgot. Be right back."

I almost ran to my office to retrieve the envelope with its mysterious contents.

CHAPTER ⚏⚏ FOURTEEN

W hat in the world?" Miss Evalina stared at me in astonishment. I'd plopped myself down in the middle of the parlor floor and dumped the contents of the envelope in front of me.

"Laura brought these by this morning on her way out of town. She found them in Clyde's safe-deposit box."

Five heads, ranging from snowy white to salt-and-pepper, leaned forward to see what I was sorting.

"They look old." Frank reached down and picked up one of the letters.

I looked through the documents, putting them in stacks. Bills of sale, receipts, letters, and other documents I couldn't determine.

"Okay, most of these are in German. We need to separate the English from the German."

"Look, this one's in German, but it has Jack Riley's name in it." Frank held it out to me. "And it's dated 1947."

I glanced over the letter. He was right. Jack Riley's name appeared three times.

I continued to look through the others. One more letter contained Jack Riley's name. I didn't recognize the signatures. Most were from someone named Frederick Heffner, with one or two from a Thomas Schmidt.

I gasped as I picked up a yellowed invoice. A fragment was torn from the document. Although it was jagged and wrinkled, the letters that were torn could very well have been 'tunnel.' I nodded with satisfaction. "Look. This would fit perfectly with the fragment Miss Aggie found in the bedpost."

The slips of paper in English proved to be appointment times. There was nothing else on them except what appeared to be an occasional street address.

"What are you going to do with these?" Miss Evalina leaned forward. "You do have a plan, don't you?"

I looked up, and her eyes stared into mine, intense and questioning. Miss Evalina wasn't going to stand for inaction.

"Yes, ma'am. First I'm going to make several copies of each item. Next, I'll take the originals to the sheriff, so he can't accuse me of withholding evidence." Of course, he wouldn't know I had copies. "Then, I'll take a copy and have them translated. After that, we'll see." I waited for her response.

Miss Evalina smiled. "Good thinking."

A wave of pleasure washed over me. I had no idea why Miss Evalina's approval meant so much to me. Maybe because she'd been such a close friend of my grandmother's. Sometimes, she even reminded me of her.

"I still think we should check out Pennington House." Miss Jane's expression lay somewhere between anger and fear. "It would be just like Aggie to send everyone on a wild-goose chase while she sneaked back to Pennington and holed up in her suite there."

I wondered if maybe searching Pennington House and grounds would be good for all of us. I didn't really expect to find Miss Aggie there, but at least we'd be doing something. I reached up and patted her hand. "Maybe we will, Miss Jane."

Her face brightened. "When?"

"I'm not sure, but soon. I promise."

She nodded, satisfied. If she'd really thought there was a chance Miss Aggie was at her old home, she wouldn't have been so willing to wait. But I understood. I was grasping at straws, too.

The phone rang. I scrambled up and hurried to the kitchen. Maybe it was Benjamin.

"Cedar Lodge."

"Hi. It's me." Phoebe sounded as dejected as I felt.

"Oh, hi Phoebe. Have you heard from the guys?"

"No, I was hoping you had."

"Not yet. But I'm sure they'll call before bedtime."

"I hope so. You don't think they'll do anything foolish, do you? I mean anything dangerous?" Her voice quivered.

"No, I'm sure they won't. Benjamin knows a lot of people on the force there. They're probably still trying to find out what the police know." But a twinge of doubt pinched at me as the memory of Benjamin and Corky, bursting into a room with a gunman, invaded my thoughts. Of course, that had been to save the rest of us. But now they were trying to save Miss Aggie.

I pushed the thought back as Phoebe's voice came through the receiver.

"I'm sure you're right." Her tone said otherwise. Phoebe was probably remembering, too. "How are the seniors holding up?"

"They have bad moments, but they're doing well, considering everything. I meant to ask, did you reschedule your dress fitting?" She'd canceled the Tuesday appointment because of Miss Aggie.

"No, I'm going to wait until we know something more."

"I don't blame you. I'm probably going to cancel mine for now, too."

Phoebe sighed. "I can't believe this has happened. I feel like I'm in a nightmare."

"I know. Same here. You can come over if you like."

"Thanks, but I'm cooking dinner for Mom and Uncle Jack."

My ears perked up. With everything that had been going on, I'd forgotten all about my questions concerning Jack Riley.

"We really need to have your uncle over for dinner again soon. Once we hear from Miss Aggie. I know the seniors would love it."

"All right. Just let me know when."

"I will. Try not to worry. I'm sure Corky will call you soon. And if I hear from Ben, I'll call and let you know."

We ended the call, and I rejoined the others in the parlor.

"Victoria, we've been talking," Miss Jane said. "We don't think we've paid close enough attention to the facts surrounding the abandoned car."

"That's right." Miss Georgina's silver curls bounced as she nodded.

"Did you have something specific in mind?"

Miss Evalina sighed. "As much as we'd like to believe Aggie is simply pulling a fast one, the evidence says otherwise."

Once again, heads bobbed in agreement.

She continued. "Aggie may have left her cell phone behind to try to fool someone. But there's no way she'd have deliberately broken the bottle of Chanel No. 5 or the clasp of her pearls."

"No way," Miss Jane agreed. "She's too frugal to waste like that. And she's had the pearls many years."

"So what are you saying?" My stomach churned.

"We have to face the fact that Aggie has likely been kidnapped again," Frank said. "Someone probably attacked her as she got out of her car. Maybe knocked her backwards. That's why some of the stuff was inside the car."

Miss Georgina gave a little cry, and to be honest, I almost did, too. To hear it admitted aloud was too much.

"Okay." Miss Jane's voice quivered a bit. "Let's go check out Pennington House. That's where they took her before."

"But Miss Jane, the Whitly Boys and Wolf are still in jail. And when they'd kidnapped Miss Aggie, it was because she could identify them as the bank robbers."

"Or so they say," Miss Jane grumbled. "How do we know the real reason didn't have something to do with Pennington House? Everything else seems to point to those stupid lost jewels."

I glanced at Miss Evalina. "Do you feel the same way?"

"I can't say that I believe Aggie is at Pennington House." She paused, then glanced around at the others. "But if Jane thinks so, it's worth checking out."

"Okay. But I don't think we should go there tonight. Benjamin said Corky checked the place, so if she's there, we need daylight to find her."

CB

Miss Georgina jumped and cried out as a boom of thunder reverberated throughout the darkened dining room, followed by a bright flash of lightning. The power had gone out a few minutes earlier, so the seniors and I sat around the dining room table, finishing our breakfast by candlelight.

"I think we should go, storm or no storm." Miss Jane seemed to be getting more agitated by the moment.

"Jane, you're being unreasonable." Miss Evalina spoke softly to her friend. "We've already determined Aggie can't be inside Pennington House, or Corky would have found her. And we absolutely cannot search the grounds with this storm raging. We'd be soaked through in two minutes, not to mention the danger of being struck by lightning."

I thanked her silently. I'd been trying to reason with Miss Jane since we'd come downstairs, but to no avail.

Miss Jane whimpered. "I know, Eva. But I can't stand to sit here doing nothing when Aggie could be. . ."

"Miss Jane, we could get the copies made and call around to try to find a translator. That way we'd at least be accomplishing something. And if you'd like, you and I can take the originals to the sheriff."

She took a deep breath. "Yes, and while we're there, I'll make him tell us what's going on. He must know more than he's saying. At least about Aggie's car and her personal belongings."

"On Saturday?" Martin scoffed.

I sighed. "The sheriff is nearly always in his office on Saturdays doing paperwork."

"Yeah, but that don't mean you can get in through the courthouse door."

I thought for a minute. "I'll call the sheriff. Maybe he'll come over here."

That settled, we finished the meal, and the ladies and I cleaned up the dining room and kitchen the best we could by candlelight. We'd have to run the dishwasher later.

As we stepped into the foyer, Frank came downstairs with an oil lamp in each hand. Martin followed with another.

"We thought we might as well play checkers or something." Frank grinned. "Keep Martin from going crazy since he can't watch his Saturday movies."

"Good idea, Frank." I smiled as Miss Evalina and Miss Georgina followed the men into the rec room. Miss Jane and I headed toward my office. We stepped inside and set our candles on the desk.

"Ack." With an embarrassed shake of the head, I glanced at her. "I don't know what I was thinking. We can't make copies until the electricity comes on."

She smacked herself on the forehead. "My goodness. I didn't think of that either."

"Oh well, at least we have phone service. I'll try to round up a translator." I grabbed a wing chair from the corner and set it by my office chair. "Here you go, Miss Jane. You sit here beside me."

I grabbed a phone book and looked up the local college. After being transferred to several departments, I finally reached a bored female voice who informed me they only taught French and Spanish and had no idea if anyone in the school could translate German documents. She then suggested I call back on Monday.

"Oh!" Miss Jane's exclamation responded to the sudden

flood of light in the room.

"Oh good. Electricity again." We smiled at each other, and I tossed the phone book in a drawer and turned on my printer. I made three copies of each document and letter and placed the copies in my safe. Then I grabbed the phone and made a call to the sheriff's office.

"Sheriff Turner."

"Hi Sheriff. This is Victoria Storm."

"Don't you know my office is closed today?"

I sighed. "Yes, I do, in fact, but apparently you're there since you answered the phone."

"Don't get smart with me. What do you want?"

"I happen to have some documents you might be interested in."

A very rude snort came through the receiver. "Okay. And just what are these important documents?"

"They happen to be letters and other paperwork that Laura Baker found in Clyde's safe-deposit box."

"And what are *you* doing with them?" At least it sounded as if he were taking me seriously now.

I explained Laura's request, leaving out the part about the copies.

He sputtered and griped, then told me to come to the back door of the courthouse and he'd let me in.

"Ready to go see Sheriff Turner?" I glanced at Miss Jane as I stuffed the originals back into the envelope.

"Ready as rain." She giggled, and I couldn't keep from responding with a giggle of my own.

Miss Jane ran upstairs to fetch her coat, and I peeked into the rec room, where the foursome now watched a John

Wayne movie. I told them where Miss Jane and I were headed then grabbed a couple of umbrellas from the stand by the front door.

I took my heavy jacket from its hook by the kitchen door and slipped it on as we went out to the garage.

Thankfully, Miss Jane didn't suggest driving her Cadillac. In this downpour, I'd have been a nervous wreck.

The square was empty except for a few cars parked in front of the café, the hardware store, and the Mocha Java. I pulled the van into a spot in front of the courthouse, and we put our umbrellas up and hurried around the sidewalk to the back entrance. The sheriff opened the door before we got up the steps. Evidently, he had been watching for us.

"Come on in before Miz Brody gets soaking wet. What do you mean by bringing her out in this kind of weather?" Hmmm. Apparently he didn't care if I got soaking wet. But at least he was showing concern for Miss Jane.

She shook her umbrella, and water splashed all over the sheriff.

"Oh, excuse me, Bobby." I grinned at her saccharin-sweet tone. "I didn't know you were so close. And incidentally, Victoria doesn't control my actions, for your information."

"Yes, ma'am."

I managed to hold back the chuckle that threatened to burst out as Miss Jane and I followed the sheriff into his office.

He motioned to the chairs in front of his desk. We all sat, and he held his hand out toward me, palm up.

Pretending not to see the hand, I laid the envelope on the chair, then took my time getting out of my wet coat, hanging it meticulously on the back of my chair.

Victoria! I scolded myself. I'd been doing so much better lately with my attitude. I handed him the envelope.

He pulled the papers out and laid them on his desk.

"What's this?" Tossing the papers aside, he grabbed a handful more and gave them a glance, then threw me an accusing look. "Is this your idea of a joke?"

"Of course not. They're in German, Sheriff."

"Oh. Well, can you read German?"

"Sorry, no. I guess you'll have to find someone to translate them."

He sucked in his bottom lip, then frowned at the documents as if they personally offended him. "Okay then. Thanks for bringing them by."

Miss Jane leaned forward. "Have you found out anything more about the suspicious circumstances of Aggie's car and personal items?"

"No, ma'am. But have you heard. . . ?" He cleared his throat, then clamped his lips together.

"Yes, Bobby, we know about the suitcase and the blood-stains."

"I'm sorry, Miz Brody. I know Miz Brow. . .Pennington-Brown was a good friend of yours."

"Was? Don't assume Aggie's dead, Bobby Turner. Because she most certainly isn't, as you'd discover if you would do your job."

His face suddenly flamed, and he coughed. "Err. . .sorry, Miz Brody. Of course she might be alive and well, probably is. Now, if you'll excuse me, I have work to do." He stood and strode over to open the door for us.

Miss Jane fumed as we drove home. "It's easier for them to conclude she's dead than to find out who took her and where."

"I know, Miss Jane. I know." But with the fresh reminder of the suitcase and the bloodstains, I couldn't keep from worrying. And I didn't see how Miss Aggie could possibly be at Pennington if her suitcase was in Jefferson City. But I wasn't about to say that to Miss Jane.

The rain didn't let up, and by late afternoon Benjamin still hadn't called back. A quick call to Phoebe revealed that she hadn't heard from Corky either.

Shortly after dinner the phone rang. I grabbed it and answered.

"Victoria, it's me." Benjamin sounded exhausted.

"What in the world is going on? Have you found out anything about Miss Aggie?"

"No, I'm sorry." He took a deep breath. "We don't know anything more than we did. But Corky's father has offered a reward, so we're hopeful someone will come forward."

I sighed. "We need to pray the reward will do some good."

"Yes, we'll do that. How is everything there?"

"The stress is starting to get to some of the seniors. But they're strong. They'll be okay."

"I love you, honey. I'll be home as soon as I can."

"I love you, too. And miss you so much. Please don't take any risks."

"I promise. Try not to worry."

"Oh. I almost forgot." I told him about Laura leaving town and the documents she'd given me.

He chuckled. "I'm proud of you for taking them to the

sheriff. It was the right thing to do."

"Yes, um, I did make copies. I'm going to try to have them translated."

"Vickie. . ."

I didn't like the exasperated tone. "I'm trying to do my part here, Benjamin, while you're doing yours in Jefferson City."

There was a short silence before he spoke. "Of course. You're right. I can't help but worry about you when I'm not there."

"I know. Just as I worry about you. But I'm trusting God to look out for you. And you need to do the same with me."

After we hung up, I went to the rec room and told Frank and Martin. The ladies had all gone to their rooms, so I went upstairs and knocked on each of their doors, giving them the news about the reward.

"Good," Miss Jane said. "That should bring someone out of the woodwork. Money usually does."

I said good night and trudged up the stairs to my third-floor apartment.

I sat in Grandma's rocker and laid my head back. Tears streamed down my cheeks. "Father, please don't let anyone hurt Miss Aggie. I couldn't bear it."

Trust Me, daughter.

The words were so strong in my spirit they were almost audible. I stayed still and listened, but nothing else came. I picked up my Bible from the side table and turned to my grandmother's favorite scripture.

"Trust in the LORD with all your heart, and lean not on your own understanding; in all your ways acknowledge Him, and He

shall direct your paths."

"I'm trying to trust You, Father. I know that You love Miss Aggie and You know exactly where she is and what is going on. I place her in Your hands once more, and this time, I'll try to leave her there. And Lord, I'll trust You to direct my path in this matter. In the name of Jesus. Amen."

CHAPTER FIFTEEN

I reached over and shut off the clock alarm, then raised my arms above my head and stretched from my toes to my shoulders. Finally, I sat up and slipped my feet into my fuzzy slippers. The room seemed a little too dark for 6:00 a.m., so I headed to the window and threw open the curtains. Just as I'd suspected, the sky was still overcast, but at least it wasn't pouring down rain like the day before.

I took a quick shower, threw on sweats, and headed downstairs. Miss Jane was wiping up the counter and humming a tune. She looked up and gave me a grin. I didn't see any food, but delicious aromas filled the air.

"You've already cooked everything and taken it to the dining room, haven't you?"

"Yes," she said, hanging the dishrag on the rack. "I woke up early and couldn't sleep, so I decided to go ahead and cook."

"Ah, it smells delicious. Is there anything left for me to do?"

"Orange juice needs pouring. The pitcher's already on the buffet."

"Miss Jane." I gave her tiny frame a squeeze then smiled.

"Have I ever told you how much I appreciate all you do to help me, especially on the weekends?"

"As a matter of fact, you have. Many times." She swished her hand at me. "Now go pour that juice. I hear the gang coming down the stairs."

I laughed and did as bidden. The seniors ambled in and began filling their plates at the sideboard, a constant chatter going on.

"Yep, I hope Whiggins don't preach two hours like he did last week." Martin frowned as he set his plate and juice on the table and sat.

"He didn't preach two hours. It was only an hour," Miss Georgina scolded, then added, "The announcements took up a lot of time."

"I like Reverend Whiggins. He tells it like it is." Miss Jane had come in from the kitchen and stood by the sideboard.

"Yeah, or tells it the way he thinks it is," Martin muttered.

The three of them went to the same church, and they'd been having similar discussions since their new preacher had taken the position last spring.

Miss Jane grabbed a plate and filled it, then sat at the end of the table. "All I can say is, if you don't like him, change churches."

"I just might do that," Martin retorted.

Okay, time for a little intervention. I turned to Miss Evalina. "How do you like House of Prayer?"

She and Frank had started attending the small, new church on the outskirts of town a few weeks ago.

She patted her lips with her napkin, her eyes alight.

"Oh Victoria, it is absolutely wonderful! The pastor is very involved in missions. You know, at one time I thought of becoming a missionary."

"Yes, I believe I do remember you mentioning it."

We got through breakfast with no more squabbles, and I breathed a sigh of relief when the seniors went upstairs to finish getting ready for church.

I loaded the dishwasher and cleaned off the table and sideboard; then I went upstairs to get ready.

I hoped Martin wasn't going to be cantankerous all day. I couldn't help but be glad he'd be having dinner with his son. Of course, Miss Jane had seemed a little skittish, too. She and Miss Georgina and I were going to the steak house in Caffee Springs after church. We planned to meet back at the lodge so we could check for messages from Benjamin and Corky before we left.

As I drove to church, I prayed for Reverend Whiggins, that his sermon would be alive and not too long, both for his sake and his congregation's.

After a very uplifting message from Pastor Carl, I drove back to the lodge. There was one message waiting from Benjamin. He only said he'd call back later.

I changed into jeans and a sweater and waited for Miss Jane and Miss Georgina to arrive. An hour later, we pulled into the parking lot at the steak house.

A western-clad server led us to a booth in the back dining room, her fringed shirt and skirt weaving us safely through heavy-laden trays borne skyward by the servers. Western music, not too loud, serenaded us as we sat on the padded seats. I sat across from the ladies, and we gave our drink orders then glanced at our menus.

A few minutes later, our server brought our glasses of iced tea and took our orders.

"Yum. It smells good in here." Miss Georgina closed her eyes and inhaled. "I love the smoky smell. It reminds me of Silver Dollar City."

Miss Jane rolled her eyes. "*Everything* reminds you of Silver Dollar City."

"That's not true," Miss Georgina retorted. "Just smoke and stuff."

"Humph." Miss Jane tilted her head as if she'd made her point.

Our food arrived in the nick of time. My small filet was cooked to perfection. The ladies had each ordered chicken-fried steak.

Miss Georgina eyed my steak and sighed. "Oh, to have my real teeth again."

"Why?" Miss Jane snapped. "I can eat steak very well with my dentures."

"Then, why don't you ever order one?"

Good for you, Miss Georgina. Stand up for yourself. Miss Jane was frowning at her.

Before she could speak, I threw her a bright smile. "How would you like to stop at Pennington House on the way home?"

"I didn't think you'd ever ask," Miss Jane said. "Let's go."

I laughed. "Let's eat first, okay?"

"That's what I meant, silly. Let's eat fast so we can leave."

A short time later we were on the blacktop back road that

led from Caffee Springs to Cedar Chapel. It also led to the uphill dirt road that would take us to Pennington House. Miss Jane sat beside me, watching closely for the turnoff.

I braked at the same time I heard Miss Georgina's gasp from the backseat.

Instead of the broken wooden sign that had marked the road for years, a black-and-white scrolled piece of art swung from a black iron hanger. The sign boasted the words PENNINGTON HOUSE.

"When did they get the new sign?" Miss Georgina voiced my thoughts.

"This is why she didn't want any of us here until the grand opening," Miss Jane said, her voice soft. "She wanted to surprise us."

"I'm surprised all right," Miss Georgina said. "Look at the road."

I turned and looked up the newly blacktopped spiral that wound its way to the top of the hill.

"Maybe we shouldn't go," Miss Georgina said with a little sob. "It almost feels like sacrilege."

"Don't talk nonsense." Miss Jane's voice trembled. "We need to search the grounds and riverbank just in case."

I took a deep breath and stepped on the gas pedal, turning onto the road. I was torn, agreeing with them both, but since we were here, I couldn't let the chance go by. Although I didn't really believe we'd find Miss Aggie here, I didn't want the idea lingering in our minds. This was probably the best way to prevent future regret.

As we wound our way up through the forest of oaks and cedars that surrounded Pennington, a myriad of thoughts raced through my mind. Miss Aggie, dirty but saucy as ever, standing in the room where she'd been imprisoned by Wolf and the Whitly boys. Benjamin grabbing a hatchet to bang down the door where the seniors and I had been locked in. That was, until Corky stopped him and handed him the key to the door—the tunnel where a murdered man had been discovered. And the day Miss Jane and I found the extension of the secret tunnel and stumbled our way into the cave, which had probably been used to hold smuggled goods.

So many secrets. Many of them still unsolved. I couldn't help but wonder how many more secrets this ancient house and grounds might hold.

We rounded the last curve, and there before us, in the midst of a lush, green lawn, stood Pennington House. But an exciting and new Pennington House. The circular drive now sported cobblestones, and an iron hitching post stood by the front walk. The building itself had been restored to what must have been its former glory, before years of neglect had taken their toll.

"Oh Jane. Look." Miss Georgina's voice held awe.

I glanced at Miss Jane. Tears streamed down her face.

"It looks just like it did when we were girls." Miss Jane's voice, too, held wonderment as she almost choked out her words.

The tall windows gleamed like diamonds, and the turret, which had fallen into dangerous disrepair, stood like a king's sentinel overlooking the estate.

"Sorry to spoil your surprise, Miss Aggie," I whispered. "But I promise we won't go inside." I opened the car door and stepped onto the cobbled stones.

A movement caught my eye, and I looked over by the side of the house. If anything had been there, it was gone now. Probably a squirrel or rabbit. But roiling unease bubbled in my stomach.

Suddenly a shot rang out. Miss Georgina shrieked.

"Get down," I yelled to the ladies, who were on the other side of the car, thankful we had our open doors to duck behind. I slid inside the car and got down as low as possible. "Get in, but keep down."

Miss Georgina wriggled onto the back floorboard and pulled the door shut.

Miss Jane eased into her seat and slammed the door, all the time leaning toward me. "What are we going to do?" she whispered.

"You stay down low. I'll try to turn the car around without getting my head shot off."

"Please, be careful."

I peeked over the steering wheel and didn't see anything. Maybe whoever shot at us was gone, but I didn't want to find out, to my sorrow, that I was wrong.

I scrunched my arm around and reached for the door handle. When I'd slammed it shut, I turned the key. As soon as the car started, I slipped the gear into DRIVE. I sat up just enough to see over the steering wheel and stepped on the gas, guiding the car around the circle drive and down the road, my eyes on the rearview mirror.

My heart lurched as an unfamiliar car shot from around the house and raced toward us.

"Victoria! A car's chasing us. Step on it!" Miss Jane shrieked.

"Get down!" I stepped on the gas and raced down the twisting road, with the other car close behind.

"Hurry, Victoria, he's gaining on us!" Miss Jane shouted.

Something ricocheted against the blacktop in front of us, and I heard the sound of something that could only be a bullet whiz by my window. Something pinged against the top of the van. In the mirror I saw the car behind us swerve, then straighten.

"Is he shooting at us?" Miss Georgina screeched. She was as flat on the floor as she could get, and her head was covered with the crocheted afghan she always kept in the van in cold weather. I hoped she didn't think it would protect her from a bullet.

"God, help us." My teeth clenched as the van careened around the curves of the road.

Miss Georgina began to pray, too.

"I can't see his face," Miss Jane yelled. "He's wearing a ski mask."

"Miss Jane. Please get down before you get hit."

The wheels spun out as I turned onto the main road without slowing down.

"He turned the other way. He's not chasing us anymore." Miss Jane flopped back and laid her head on the headrest, breathing hard.

Miss Georgina popped up and climbed onto the seat. I could hear her heavy breathing.

"Okay, everyone fasten your seat belts because I'm not slowing down until we get to town."

I let out a sigh of relief when we passed the Cedar Chapel city-limit sign. Slowing down, I drove to the square and turned toward the courthouse. I parked, and we all jumped out and speed walked into the building.

The locked door brought us to our senses.

"Oh no, it's Sunday. They're closed," Miss Georgina moaned.

"C'mon." I led the way around to the back. Sure enough. The sheriff's car was parked in the back lot.

I ran up the steps and started pounding on the door. Why didn't I have the sense to get a cell phone? I could call his office. I pounded harder. "Sheriff, please open up!"

Tom's eyes widened as he stuck his head around the corner and saw us. We must have looked pretty scary. He darted back inside. A minute later, the sheriff opened the door.

"What is it now, Victoria?" he blustered.

I pushed Miss Jane and Miss Georgina through the door then shoved my way in. Even if the shooter did go the other way on the blacktop road, he could have turned and followed us.

The three of us stood panting while the sheriff and his deputy stared.

"What's wrong?" By now, the sheriff looked concerned.

"Someone. . .shot at us out at the Pennington place," I said, between gasps.

Sheriff Turner's lips pressed together in a hard, flat line. "Come on in my office."

☙

Gratefully, I accepted the glass of water Tom passed to me after he'd given the elderly ladies theirs. The sheriff hadn't said anything since we'd sat in the chairs around his desk. For once he seemed truly concerned.

Finally, my pulse stopped racing, and my breathing slowed to near normal. Miss Jane and Miss Georgina had calmed down as well.

"Now then." The sheriff's calm tone of voice was devoid of the sarcasm it usually held when he spoke to me. "Please start at the beginning, and tell me what happened."

"We were. . ."

"We went. . ."

"The reason. . ."

As we all began to speak at once, Sheriff Turner held up his hand. "One at a time, please. Why don't you go first, Miz Wilder?"

She looked at him in surprise. In fact, we all did. Everyone in town called Miss Georgina, well, Miss Georgina. She preferred it. I wasn't sure why.

"All right." She folded her hands primly on her lap. "We went to the steak house in Caffee Springs after church. That is, Victoria, Jane, and me. On the way home, we decided to stop at Pennington and search the grounds in case the kidnappers took Aggie there."

The sheriff took a deep breath, and his face tightened.

At the change in his countenance, Miss Georgina's face reddened. "Oh dear. Jane, you tell him." She threw me an apologetic look.

"It's okay," I murmured. "We didn't do anything wrong."

"Don't you say a word, Bobby Turner," Miss Jane said. "We found Aggie there before, and who's to say she's not there now?"

"Dane Pennington searched every inch of the place, Miz Brody. Miz Pennington-Brown's not there."

"But did he search the grounds? Or the riverbank?" she snapped.

"No, he didn't, but Tom and I did. She's nowhere on the Pennington property." As she started to say something, he added, "Including the caves. We checked them all."

"Oh. You should have told us." She tossed her head.

"No, ma'am. I *shouldn't* have told you, because we don't advertise our investigating practices to the public."

Wow, he actually stood up to her. I decided I'd better interrupt before Miss Jane gave him an earful.

"Anyway, we pulled up to the house. When we got out, I thought I saw movement at the side of the house, but when I turned and looked, there was nothing." I licked my lips. "Then a shot rang out. Luckily both car doors were still open, so we managed to stay low and get into the van."

"Where were the ladies sitting?" Sheriff asked.

"Miss Georgina was in the back, down on the floor, and Miss Jane was in the front passenger seat, leaning over. I started the car and took off around the drive and down the road."

"And you never did see anyone?"

"I'm getting to that. Just as I pulled onto the road, a car shot out from around the house and started after us. I stepped on the gas, but he was gaining on me."

"So you did see the shooter?"

"No, but Miss Jane did."

He turned to her. "Can you give me a description, Miz Brody?"

She frowned. "He was wearing a ski mask."

"And?"

"And nothing. That's all I saw."

He sighed loudly. "Okay, can anyone describe the car?"

"I didn't recognize it," I said. "And it happened so fast I couldn't tell what make or model it was. It was dark, maybe dark green, but I can't be sure. With the overcast sky and the shadows from the trees, it could have been black or dark blue.

"When we got to the main road, he went the other direction. We didn't see him after that."

"Okay, and you're sure what you heard was a shot?"

"Oh, I almost forgot. He started shooting again while he was chasing us. Several bullets hit the van."

He jumped up. "Why didn't you tell me that when you got here? Let's go take a look."

Miss Georgina jumped up, but Miss Jane remained seated. "Sit down, Georgina. Let them go look without us."

Miss Georgina sank back onto the chair, a look of relief on her face.

I trailed after the sheriff and Tom. They were already out the courthouse door. When I got to the van, they were inspecting it carefully.

"I don't see any signs of these bullets that were trying to get you," Tom said, rolling his eyes. It wasn't the first trace of sarcasm I'd ever heard from him.

"Lucky for you, your shooter, if there was one, wasn't very good. But at least you didn't get killed." He winked at me. Then his expression changed, and he reached over to the top of the van, running his finger over a tiny area.

"Hey, Chief," he called. "I think one of them bullets must have grazed the top here. There's a dent. No hole, but it's kinda chewed up."

"Tom, go inside and get me an evidence bag." Sheriff

Turner's voice sounded a little shaky. "Victoria, come over here."

He was leaning over the back taillight. I inhaled sharply when I saw it. The red glass was shattered, and something was embedded in the metal behind it.

"I'm really sorry." Sheriff Turner's voice was sincere. "I thought you were exaggerating. But I think you've got us a piece of evidence here. A pretty little piece of evidence in the form of a bullet."

CHAPTER ⛩ SIXTEEN

I groaned and reached over to turn off the alarm. It kept ringing. Groggy and disoriented, I stared at the numbers, which read 2:46 a.m. It rang again. *No, no, that's the telephone*. I grabbed the receiver. Who would be calling this time of the morning?

"Hello," I mumbled.

"Victoria, Sarah's run away." Mabel's voice bordered on hysteria. "She's not anywhere in the house, and her suitcase is gone."

Wide awake now, I shot up and swung my legs over the side of the bed.

"Mabel." Wails from the other end told me she hadn't heard. I raised my voice. "Mabel, calm down. Have you called the sheriff?"

She gasped. "Oh my goodness. I'll do that now. Your number was the only one I could think of."

"Okay. Do you have any idea why she left or where she might have gone?"

"She was upset because her daddy hasn't called her in over a week. She cried at bedtime and said she wanted to go home. I felt so helpless."

"How long has she been gone, and did she have any money with her?" The bus only made pickups in Cedar Chapel at noon and midnight. I shivered at the thought of little Sarah standing in front of the deserted general store in the dark, waiting for the bus.

"I don't know when she left. I woke up a few minutes ago, thirsty. I got up for a glass of water and noticed her door open, so I went in. Her piggy bank was on the floor. . . broken, but it only had two or three dollars in change."

"All right. Call the sheriff and report this, and I'll go look for her. If I find her, I'll bring her home. If not, I'll be over anyway."

I threw on jeans and a sweater, grabbed my down coat and ran downstairs, hoping I didn't wake the seniors.

I had no idea if Sarah had been gone for several hours or just a few minutes. Deciding to search the road leading from town to Mabel's farm first, I headed that way. As I turned onto the dark, rutted road, my chest tightened within me. "God, please let her be all right, and help me to find her."

There was no sign of her on the road, so I went back into town. On a hunch, I drove through town to the blacktop road that led to Branson.

I'd gone about a mile when I saw a small, dark form, a little ways down the road. She was hunched against the wind, her heavy suitcase bouncing against the road, as she dragged it behind her.

She turned as I pulled up beside her. When she saw it was me, she turned back and began to trudge down the road. I drove slowly beside her until she stopped. Dropping the suitcase, she stormed around to my window and glared at me, her hands on her tiny hips.

"Leave me alone! I'm going home to see Dad." She lifted her hand and wiped it against her eyes, leaving a smudge of dirt. I looked at her hands and saw they were dirty and scraped up. She must have fallen.

"Sarah, would you get in please, so we can talk?"

"No, you'll take me straight back to Grandma's, and I told you I'm going home."

"Sweetheart, I just want to talk to you. And it's cold with the window down."

A shiver went through her small body as uncertainty filled her eyes. "Okay, but you're not gonna change my mind."

She walked around and yanked open the door, then climbed up onto the seat. "Man, this seat is almost as high as my dad's truck seat."

"I know. It's old, and I really need to replace it soon."

Another shiver passed over her body. I grabbed a crocheted afghan from the backseat, thankful that Miss Georgina always kept one in the van in cold weather.

"Here, you may as well warm up some while we talk, okay?" She didn't protest, so I tucked it around her.

"Sweetie, do you want to tell me about it?"

"I'm worried about my daddy. She gave a little sighing hiccup. "He promised he'd call me every few days, and it's been way longer than that."

"Maybe he's been busy." The minute the words were out of my mouth, I knew the excuse wouldn't fly with her.

Sure enough, a scowl wrinkled her face. "Day and night? Too busy to call and just say hi to me?"

"What do you think the reason is?" Maybe it would work best if I let her do the talking. I seemed to be putting my foot in my mouth more than anything.

"I don't know. Maybe he's hurt or something. He could be in the hospital and too sick to ask anyone to call me or Grandma." Her lips trembled, and she scrunched her nose against the tears that threatened to spill.

Déjà vu hit me hard, and memories assailed me. Grandma, rocking me while I cried heart-wrenching sobs. Then, when I was a little older, excuses I made because Mom and Dad hadn't written or called in what seemed to me like weeks. I swallowed and tried to focus on Sarah. I'd survived the heartache. She would, too, if that's the way it had to be. But maybe there really was a satisfactory reason that Sarah's father hadn't called.

"Sweetheart, has your grandma tried to call him?"

"Yes. Twice, but he didn't answer his phone."

I leaned forward. "I tell you what. If you'll come back to your grandma's house, I promise to try to find your dad for you."

"Tonight?"

I grinned. "Do you realize what time it is?"

"Late?"

"Almost 3:30. But I'll get on it tomorrow. And I'll find out why your dad hasn't called. I promise. Deal?"

She studied my face, then nodded. She stuck out a grimy little paw. "Deal."

I shook her hand. "How about I help you with that suitcase?"

"Nah. I can get it." She hopped out and grabbed the long

handle on the suitcase. She pushed and shoved it into the backseat, then got back in, breathing hard.

I reached over and squeezed her hand. "Okay, I guess we're ready."

We pulled up in front of Mabel's house ten minutes later. She and Bob Turner stood by the patrol car. When she saw Sarah, she threw her hands up and came running.

Sarah let her grandmother hug her tightly. "Oh Sarah, baby. What were you thinking? I was worried 'bout to death."

"Sorry. I didn't mean to worry you, Grandma." She reached up a finger and wiped the tears from Mabel's cheek. "I really am sorry. Please don't cry."

"Okay, my angel, I won't cry anymore." She threw me a look that held fathoms of gratitude. "How can I thank you?"

"Oh, you don't need to thank me. Sarah made the decision to come home. All I did was give her a ride." I winked, then turned to the sheriff, who'd walked over and stood beside me.

"Good work." His eyes held a glimmer of respect in which I sort of basked. Most of the time he let me know, in his eyes, I was a big pain in the neck.

"Thanks, Sheriff. But I didn't do much. It was logical she'd head in that direction."

"My thoughts, too. Was just getting ready to head that way myself." He grinned. "I guess we were on the same wavelength."

"Uh-huh. As they say, great minds think alike."

He chortled. "I guess that's right. Okay, guess I'm not needed here." He got in his car and pulled away.

"Won't you come in for coffee?" Mabel called to me. "I've got donuts, too."

"No, thanks. I'd better get back to the lodge." I leaned over and looked in Sarah's eyes. "I won't forget."

She nodded. "Okay. Guess I'll see you in the morning."

"I'll look forward to that. Maybe I'll even have news for you by the time you get home from school. But don't be disappointed if it takes a little longer than that."

I got the phone number from Mabel and the name of the plant where her son worked.

When I got to the lodge, I tiptoed in and up the stairs. Not a sound came from any of the rooms, and I breathed a sigh of relief as I went up to my apartment.

I crawled into bed without changing. "Thank You, Lord, that Sarah is safe and in her own bed. I need Your help to keep my promise about her dad."

The alarm clock woke me. I stretched and yawned, wishing I could turn over and go back to sleep. A quick shower revived me.

When I got downstairs, the sound of singing came from the kitchen, and I walked in to see a smiling Mabel. Sarah was finishing her oatmeal and toast. She ran to brush her teeth, and before she headed out the door with her backpack snugly against her back, she turned and gave me a wink, then mouthed, "Don't forget."

℆

I stood on the front porch and waved as Miss Jane's Cadillac backed out into the street. Miss Georgina waved back, and then Miss Jane followed Frank's truck down the street. I went back inside and straight to my office. I wanted to call the college, but I knew I needed to keep my promise to Sarah first.

I punched in the number of the plant where Mabel's son worked. A friendly voice answered, "Mason's Metal Works."

"Hello, my name is Victoria Storm. I'm trying to locate Bobby Carey. He is an employee there."

"One moment, please. I'll transfer you to his department."

Country music screamed into my ear, and I jerked the receiver away. Good grief. I liked country music sometimes. After all, it was Grandpa's favorite. Hillbilly music, he'd called it. But it was ridiculous the way they had it turned up.

"Hello, this is Dave," the deep voice boomed, and I quickly put the receiver back to my ear.

"Hello, I'm trying to locate Bobby Carey. Is he there? And may I speak to him please?"

"Who's calling?" Was that belligerence? Or something else? Wariness, maybe?

"My name is Victoria Storm, and I'm calling for his mother and daughter. They haven't heard from him in a while and are getting worried."

"Sorry, we haven't heard from him either. He ain't been to work for days and isn't answering his phone. If you find him, tell him if he wants his job he needs to call in."

"Yes, I will. And if you hear from him, will you please ask him to call his mother?"

"Sure. What's the phone number?"

"He knows the number. Thank you."

I put the receiver down and leaned back, my fingers drumming the wooden arm of my desk chair. I hadn't expected this. Now what?

I toyed with the idea of calling Benjamin. But the very fact that he hadn't yet called made me hesitate. I didn't want to interrupt if he was on the verge of finding answers.

I picked the phone back up and punched in Bobby's cell phone number. After two rings, I was switched to his voice mail. I left a message for him to call me or his mother and hung up.

I scrolled through my rolodex until I found the number of the university in Springfield. The receptionist put me through to the Foreign Language Department.

"Yes, how may I help you?" The male voice sounded polite but hurried.

"Hello, my name is Victoria Storm. I'm attempting to find someone who translates German."

"German, you say? Our Professor Johannsen would be the person to talk to. I'll switch you over."

"Thank you."

"Professor Johannsen. May I help you?" The accent was definitely German, and I sighed with relief.

I gave him my name and told him what I was in need of.

"You say these documents and letters date back to the 1940s?" His voice sounded charged with excitement.

"Yes sir. Some of them are mid–World War II, but most are after 1945."

"Very interesting. I would be delighted to translate for you. Can you meet me here in my office around one o'clock this afternoon?"

I calculated the time and decided I'd be able to leave the letters and be back here before Sarah got home from school.

"Yes, I'll be there. Thank you for meeting with me so promptly."

"Not at all. I'll see you at one." He disconnected the call.

I went to the kitchen, where Mabel stood over the chopping block cutting onions into quarters. She looked up hopefully.

I shook my head, wondering if I should tell her about the conversation with the man at the plant. I knew she'd worry more, but she needed to know.

"I'm sorry. I spoke to someone in his department. They haven't heard from him in several days. Can you think of any friends or relatives who might know something about his whereabouts?"

"Yes. There was a couple Bobby and Carol used to talk about. I never met them. Now what was their names?" She thought for a moment, shaking her head, then her eyes lit. "Borden. Their last name was Borden. He was Tom, and she was Nancy. Will that help?"

"I'm not sure, but we can try. I don't suppose Sarah would know their phone number or address?"

"I don't know. I'll ask her when she gets home from school."

"Okay, but I'm going to call information. Maybe we can find out something before Sarah gets home."

I returned to my office and called long-distance information, giving them the city and the names.

Soon, an automated voice said, "Please hold for the number."

I grabbed a pen and sticky note and wrote it down. Then, on a deep breath, I punched in the number.

"Hello?" Expectation filled the woman's voice.

"Hello, my name is Victoria Storm. Am I speaking to Nancy Borden?"

"Ye–yes."

"Mrs. Borden, I'm searching for Bobby Carey. I understand you and your husband used to be friends with him and his wife, Carol."

"Yeah. What about it?"

"I'm trying to find Bobby. Would you by any chance know his whereabouts?"

A short laugh sounded through the earpiece. "If I did, I'd know my husband's whereabouts."

"Your husband is missing, too?"

"I don't know about missing. He and Bobby left here yesterday, three sheets to the wind, if you know what I mean. I haven't heard from them since."

Nausea gripped me. How was I going to tell his mother about this? And what could we tell Sarah?

"So Bobby was with you and your husband yesterday?"

She laughed, and when she spoke, her words slurred. "Bobby's been here since last week. Came over all depressed. I couldn't blame him much. That wife of his, dumping him and the kid the way she did." She inhaled and, after a few seconds, exhaled loudly. Then wracking coughs assaulted my ears. "Sorry, these cigs are gonna be the death of me. Anyway, Tom bought a couple of six-packs, and that was just the beginning. Bobby went and bought hard liquor, and one thing led to another. They've been drinking for days. Like I said, I don't know where they are. They'll likely come dragging in sooner or later."

"Thank you, Mrs. Borden. Would you mind taking down my phone number?"

"Sure, just a minute." I could hear her scrambling around.

"Okay, I'm ready. What's the number?"

I spoke slowly so she'd be sure to hear it correctly, then had her repeat it back to me. I suspected she'd had a few drinks herself. "If he does return, will you ask him to please call me or his mother?"

"Sure. I'll tell him."

I went back to the kitchen. Mabel was seasoning whole fryers to roast. Dread and fear filled her eyes when she looked at me. "What is it? My boy's not dead, is he?"

"No, no. Nothing like that. In fact, I have information he was alive and well yesterday. I've left your phone number and mine with a message for him to call." I gave her a bright smile.

Her eyes narrowed. "Don't lie to me, Victoria. There's something you're not telling me."

I never have been good at keeping secrets. Case in point, the way Mrs. Miller always got the family secrets out of me.

"Okay, I'm sorry. I wanted to spare you, but you're his mother, and I haven't the right to keep this from you."

She sat, eyes straight ahead, as I gave her the information I'd gotten from Nancy Borden.

Tears filled her eyes, and she reached for a tissue and blotted them away. "Well, I didn't expect this. I never knew Bobby was a drinker. I guess it just got to be too much for him. He was so crazy about Carol. Don't know what I'll tell Sarah, though."

"I'm sure he'll be fine. He'll get over this. It's probably a one-time thing."

"I hope so. Thanks for hunting him down." She picked up one of the roasters and placed it in a large pan, then did the same with the other. She covered them both with the lid and placed the pan in the refrigerator. Apparently, the conversation was over.

"Okay. I have to run over to Springfield and meet someone on business. I should be back before Sarah gets here. If Benjamin calls, ask him to please call me back."

I went upstairs to change. How much should we tell Sarah that would let her know her father was safe without thinking he didn't care about her enough to call her? I said a quick prayer as I changed into dress slacks and jacket. I hadn't been on a university campus since I'd graduated ten years ago.

I retrieved a set of the documents from my filing cabinet. As I made the hour-and-a-half drive to Springfield, varying emotions fought inside me. Sadness and heartbreak for Sarah's situation, and a tinge of excitement about the documents.

CHANGER ⫟⫟ ⫟⫟⫟ SEVENTEEN

I pulled my van into the visitors parking area. A little overwhelmed by the massive campus, I went searching for the building that housed the Foreign Language Department. Thanks to a friendly young student, within a few minutes I was ushered into Professor Johannsen's office. Immediately, the smell of furniture polish and old leather wafted up my nostrils.

The professor, who appeared to be in his late sixties or early seventies, sat behind a massive oak desk.

When he saw me standing there, he stood and gave a slight bow, then motioned to the wine-colored leather chair in front of his desk. "Please sit down, Miss Storm. I am Professor Johannsen."

When I was seated, he returned to his chair. "You have something to show me?"

"Yes." I reached into my oversize bag and took out the envelope in which I'd stuffed the copies. I handed them across the desk to him.

With a nod in my direction, he shook the documents onto his desk. He picked up one at random. Then another.

"Hmm. These two are merely receipts for merchandise."

He gave me a questioning glance.

"Yes, but I still need them translated. Please don't leave anything out."

"Very well." He appeared disappointed. I hoped he'd find something that would interest or even intrigue him. If I was right about Clyde's involvement in crime, I was pretty sure he would.

He smiled and stood up. "I'll have my assistant give you a receipt for these and will call you when the translations are complete."

"All right." I stood, too, since I was obviously dismissed. "Do you have any idea when you'll have them done?"

He frowned. "I have a banquet to attend tonight. I might perhaps have time to at least start them tomorrow afternoon. But my assistant will call you."

"Very well. Thank you, Professor." I reached my hand across the desk, and he took it in his massive one.

I left the campus feeling like I'd been kicked out of his office. To soothe my feelings, I went through a coffee shop drive-through and treated myself to a caramel cappuccino.

I pulled into the driveway at Cedar Lodge at two forty-five, proud of myself for making good time.

Mabel was putting the chickens into the oven as I walked in.

"My son called." Excitement filled her voice, and a wide smile graced her face. "A few minutes after you left. He's fine. He apologized and said he'll call Sarah tonight. He said he had no idea so much time had passed since he went to the Bordens' house. He's not used to drinking, you know."

"I'm so happy to hear that. Sarah will be ecstatic."

"He said he was going to call his boss right away and make sure he still had a job. And guess what?" Her face was radiant.

"What? It must be great."

"He got saved this morning." She put her hands to her face, but I could still see the tears that were raining down her cheeks. "I've been praying for him for years. This morning, he woke up on a cot in a mission. Tom was there, too, but he was still asleep. Bobby went downstairs to see what was going on. Breakfast was being served, so he sat down to eat. A man came over and began to talk to him about the love of God. Bobby said suddenly the words the man was speaking went right into his heart, and he repented right then and there. Then the man led him in a prayer to accept Jesus as his Savior. Oh, my." She reached for a tissue then wiped her wet face.

"That's wonderful, Mabel. God is so good." I gave her a hug. "We were worried about what to tell Sarah, and all the while God was speaking to Bobby's heart."

I went up to change into my jeans, praising God all the while. "Thank You, Lord. Your way is so perfect. And You have all the answers. Thank You for the joy that little girl will experience today. Please comfort Bobby and keep him strong. And Lord, I ask that what You've done for Bobby, You'll do for his wife, Carol, and the Bordens. In Jesus' name. Amen."

When I got back downstairs, Sarah was in the kitchen, laughing and chattering like she'd never had a care in the world. I walked into the kitchen, and she stopped speaking. The look she gave me was one of total joy. When she grabbed me around the waist and hugged me tight, a strange but thrilling sensation bubbled in my chest.

"You kept your promise. You found my daddy for me." She continued to hang on, and suddenly my arms wrapped around her, and I hugged back.

Finally, I leaned over, brushed her bangs back, and looked into her eyes. "It was really God who did it, honey. He just used me as a tool to get the job done. See how much He loves you, to do that for you?"

A look of awe washed over her face. "God did it for me?"

"Yes, for you and your grandmother and for your daddy."

A beautiful smile appeared on her face. "Cool. He sure loves me a lot, doesn't He?"

The phone rang, and Mabel, with tears still flowing, went to answer, then handed it to me.

"Hi, honey." I knew from Benjamin's voice he had some good news. "Guess who just turned up at Simon's house?"

I gasped. "Miss Aggie?"

"The one and only. Fit to be tied because Simon had offered a reward for her. Said she felt like a display in a museum when she was only taking care of some business." He chortled.

I joined him, laughter bubbling up. Miss Aggie was safe. "When is everyone coming home?"

"Corky and I are leaving now. Miss Aggie is staying on a day or so to talk to the police about a few things and to visit with Simon. Then he'll bring her home."

"I have to go tell the seniors. Come by when you get to town."

"Oh, believe me, sweetheart, I will. I can't wait to hold

you in my arms. I love you, baby."

"I love you, too."

I ran up the stairs and called out, "Hey, everyone, Miss Aggie's coming home!"

Miss Jane's door was the first to fly open. "What did you say? Aggie's home?"

By then all the seniors were out in the hall.

"Did you say Aggie's home?" Miss Georgina's face was bright enough to light the whole house.

I laughed. "No, but she's safe, and she's coming home in a day or two. I just got off the phone with Benjamin."

We all trooped downstairs and filed into the parlor, where they insisted I tell them about the call from Benjamin, word for word.

"Can you beat it?" Martin frowned. "Here everyone was worried half to death thinking she'd been killed, and she gets mad because her nephew reported her missing and offered a reward. Women."

Frank winked at him and placed his arm around Miss Evalina. "Aw, Martin. Women are great. Especially my Evie. Maybe if you had one of your own, you wouldn't be so snappy."

Miss Evalina blushed and patted her husband's hand. "Aggie is probably embarrassed that she went off without thinking. We all know she's a little absentminded sometimes. But I don't think she set out to deliberately make us worry."

A tap on the parlor door drew my attention. Mabel stood there smiling. It was a joyful day in more ways than one.

"I'm leaving now, Victoria. I put everything on the steam table. The salad is in the refrigerator, and dessert is already on the buffet."

"Thanks, Mabel, and I'm so glad everything turned out well with Bobby." I turned to the seniors. "I want to say good-bye to Sarah."

She was in the backyard giving Buster a farewell hug. They'd become great friends. In fact, when she was around, I might as well not be. And he used to be stuck to me like glue.

When I walked out the door, she came running, a big grin on her face. "See you tomorrow."

"Okay, see you tomorrow." When they drove away, I went into the yard with Buster. "Want to stay out a little longer, boy?"

I'd been making him stay in the yard in the daytime and in the basement at night. He was such a monster dog. An oversize puppy, really.

He rubbed against my leg, and I scratched his head. "Oh, why not? Come on inside."

He followed me into the parlor and plopped down in front of the fireplace, tolerating the pats and affectionate murmurs the seniors poured on him.

A big grin split his shaggy face. My heart turned over, and I gave him a hug before I flopped down on my chair. What a perfect day.

⚘

I was waiting on the front-porch swing with Buster asleep by my feet. Benjamin's truck pulled up and parked in front of the lodge. I ran to meet him and snuggled into his arms, welcoming the familiar scent of his aftershave. Buster nudged us once, then went back to his spot by the swing.

"How long have you been waiting out here in the cold?" He took my hands and rubbed them.

"It's not that cold. Only fifty degrees tonight. And I've only been outside a half hour or so. The seniors were so excited that they stayed up late. I knew you'd be arriving anytime, so I came out to wait. We can go inside if you'd rather."

"Nah. Let's sit on the swing. My favorite place."

"Mine, too, as long as you're here with me."

We sat, and he pulled me close. I leaned my head on his shoulder. The world seemed so right when Ben was near and so wrong when he wasn't.

"I thought Corky might stop by with you."

"No, I dropped him by Phoebe's. That's where he left his truck. He's probably still there."

I laughed. "I'm sure. Oh, by the way, Jack Riley's back. He said he'd been away on business."

He raised an eyebrow and grinned.

"Uh-uh." I put a finger to his lips. "Don't you dare say 'I told you so,' because I'm still not convinced he's innocent."

He shook his head. "Vickie, Vickie."

"Never mind. Tell me about Miss Aggie."

"I don't really know anything more than I told you on the phone. She was rip-roaring mad, though."

"I hope she'll tell us what's going on. She didn't go to Jefferson City merely to sightsee. She's up to something."

"You may be right." He bent his head and nuzzled my neck, sending a thrill clear to my toes.

"Behave yourself."

"I'm tired of behaving myself. Let's neck." A wide yawn interrupted his ardor.

I laughed. "I think what you need is to go home and get some sleep."

"Yeah, I know. When are we going to finish making plans for the wedding?"

"Let's talk about it when Miss Aggie gets home and this mystery about Clyde's death is solved."

He groaned. "It's always something."

I reached over and brushed a lock of his sandy hair from his forehead. "We don't want an unsolved murder hanging over us during the wedding and our honeymoon, do we?"

He sat up and took my hand. "I guess you're right. But I don't even want to think of postponing our wedding day."

"Neither do I, but I don't think it'll come to that. We may be closer than we think to solving Clyde's murder."

He narrowed his eyes. "What do you mean? Have you been up to something?"

"Not really, but I think the documents Laura brought me are going to reveal something."

I told him about the references to Jack Riley in some of the letters and then admitted I'd taken them to be translated.

"I asked you to take them to the sheriff."

"But I did. I simply made copies first. You know he wouldn't have told us anything."

"Does he know you have copies?"

"No, but what difference does that make? I didn't break any law, and I gave him the originals, so I'm not withholding evidence."

A muscle jumped beside his mouth, and then he chuckled. "No, I suppose you're not."

I leaned over and pressed my lips briefly against his. "Good night."

"You running me off?"

"Uh-huh. You need to get some rest."

He stretched and yawned again. "Sorry."

I laughed. "You don't need to be sorry. I know you're not bored. How could you be? You're with me."

"Okay. That's very true."

"So go home. And don't try to work tonight, okay?"

"Yes, ma'am." He jumped up. "One more for the road, okay?"

I laughed and put my arms around his neck. "I love you."

He bent toward me, and I closed my eyes. His lips pressed against mine, and when he raised his head, I leaned against his chest.

"I love you, too, baby." His voice was hoarse. "G'night."

"Good night. Come to dinner tomorrow?"

"I thought you'd never ask."

After he'd gone, I filled Buster's water bowl and put him in the basement, then turned off the lights and went upstairs.

A few minutes later, I crawled between cool, soft sheets and sank into my down pillows. "Thank You, Lord. For everything."

With a smile on my lips, I closed my eyes.

ରୁ

I sat up, heart pounding, and glanced at my alarm. Only six o'clock. A scream pierced the air, and a crash reverberated through the house. What in the world? I jumped up and raced across the room, flinging the door open. I raced down the first flight of stairs and headed down the hall, flying past startled seniors with their heads stuck out their doors. I bolted down the next flight of stairs and tripped on the bottom step, almost losing my balance.

A black-and-white streak disappeared down the foyer and into the great hall. Buster thundered after it, barking fiercely. My feet hit the bottom stair and skidded off. I landed on my behind, just as Sarah ran by, her screams as loud as Buster's barks. Mabel appeared in the kitchen doorway, her eyes wide.

I jumped up and ran to the great hall. The cat crouched on the mantel, snarling down at Buster, while Sarah, who'd grabbed Buster's collar, hung on to keep him from trying to climb up after the offender.

"Sarah!" I shouted to make myself heard over the snarls and barks. "How did that cat get in here?"

She whipped around. "Oh, did we wake you up?"

"Uh, yeah."

She looked down at my feet. "You're barefoot."

I put my hands on my hips and tapped my foot. "Did you bring the cat inside?"

"Yes. . .and no."

"Explain, please."

She scrunched her face up as though in deep thought. "I was playing with Fluffy and a ball of string out in the front yard. When I came in, I guess I must have accidentally let the string hang down, and Fluffy followed me inside, trying to grab it."

"Oh, so you really didn't mean to use the string as bait to get the cat in the house?" I glared.

"Well, okay. I thought it might be fun to see what Buster would do." She smiled sweetly and gave me an oh-so-innocent look. "I'm sorry. I never meant for them to make so much noise and wake you up."

"You know what? You remind me of a boy I used to know. His name was Benjamin. One day he painted my dog and put him on top of the preacher's toolshed. But of course, he didn't mean any harm either."

"Oh." Her eyes widened. "Was it Mr. Grant? That Benjamin?"

I could tell she was impressed instead of thinking it was awful, so what was I to do?

"Yeah, that's the one. Okay, you hang onto Buster, and I'll see if I can get Fluffy out of here."

I walked over to the fireplace and eyed the cat. By now, he'd stretched out on the mantel and was busy licking his fur. I reached over and laid my hand on his back. He just looked at me, so I picked him up and carried him out, Buster's furious barks following us all the way to the back door.

I deposited him on Mrs. Miller's front lawn and went back inside. "Okay, Sarah. Do you think you can put Buster in the backyard without him taking off after the cat again?"

"Sure, all I have to do is put his leash on and hang onto it." Which she proceeded to do.

Mabel eyed me. "Better get dressed before you catch a cold running around in your pajamas and bare feet."

I grinned. "I guess I'd better. I haven't showered yet either." I headed for the stairs.

"Miss Victoria."

I turned. Sarah stood in the kitchen doorway, uncertainty written on her face.

"Back home, my best friend's name is Victoria. I called her Torey." She blinked her eyes, fast. "Is it okay if I call you Miss Torey?"

I inhaled sharply, then swallowed. "Sweetheart, I'd be

honored."

She grinned. "Okay, I gotta go catch the bus. Bye, Miss Torey."

My heart swelled inside me as she grabbed her backpack and ran out the back door.

Mabel turned and smiled. "She really likes you."

"Yeah, she does, doesn't she?" With a light step, I climbed the two flights of stairs to my room. Why in the world was I so happy just because a child seemed to like me? Oh, I didn't have time to think about that now. But, whatever the reason, it was a great feeling.

As I stepped out of the shower, the phone rang.

"Miss Storm? This is Trudy Newton, Johannsen's assistant."

"Yes, Miss Newton?"

"The professor has finished translating your documents and can see you in his office at two o'clock this afternoon, if that's convenient for you."

"Yes, that's quite convenient. I'll be there."

Excitement clutched at my stomach as I dressed and went downstairs. This day might prove to be as wonderful as the day before. It was certainly starting out that way.

CHAPTER ⫿⫿⫿ EIGHTEEN

Breakfast was over, and the seniors were getting ready to head out to the center for bingo and fellowship. I glanced around, my eyes resting on Miss Jane. "Anyone want to go to Springfield with me today?"

Miss Jane's face turned pink. "I promised to have lunch with someone at the center."

"Oh, okay." Hmm. Miss Jane wasn't one to blush. Now what was going on?

Miss Georgina spoke up. "I'll go with you."

I looked at her in surprise. She seldom went anywhere without Miss Jane.

"Great. My appointment isn't until two. We'll have lunch first."

"If you want to, we could take one loop around Silver Dollar City. They open at ten today, so we'd have plenty of time."

"I'd love it. Sounds like fun."

An hour later we were on the road to Branson. "It's a perfect day for it. I'm so glad the sun is out."

"Me, too." Her face glowed with excitement. I was happy it had worked out this way. Miss Jane and I often took off on little adventures together, and before Miss Evalina was married, the two of us occasionally went somewhere. But this was a first-time jaunt for Miss Georgina and me.

We arrived on the outskirts of Branson, passed a little café with a sign that always made me drool.

"Look, Miss Georgina. They have Italian beef sandwiches. We need to stop there sometime."

She giggled. "You say that every time we pass it. By the time we head back out of town, we're so stuffed no one even thinks about food."

"Yeah. I know." I drove down the wide highway into town, admiring the hills and valleys until we came to our turnoff to Silver Dollar City.

"Oh look, Victoria. They have the autumn decorations all around the sign."

Corn shocks and pumpkins adorned the grass around the Silver Dollar City sign, as well as other fall ornamentation. Childhood memories always came flooding back when I reached this point. Grandma and Grandpa brought me here often when I was a child, and many times, Benjamin came with us.

"Wow, it looks great, doesn't it?" The parking areas weren't very full this early in the day, so we got a spot near the tram and trolley stop and walked the few steps.

"Here comes a trolley now. We won't need to wait."

She was right. The trolley did its U-turn and stopped in front of us.

The driver tipped his green cap as we climbed aboard and sat in the open vehicle. "Good morning, ladies. Looks like you're the only ones riding this trip."

The wind, which hadn't seemed cold while we were standing, whipped against us as the trolley drove the short distance to the park. I cupped my hands over my ears to shield them.

Five minutes later we arrived at the entrance.

We went through the open ticket booths where Miss Georgina presented her season pass to a lady in a long pioneer-type dress, and I paid my one-day admission fee and went through the revolving gate.

Inside the park, I stopped and closed my eyes, inhaling deeply of wood smoke, cinnamon, and barbecue.

Miss Georgina giggled. "You do the same thing I do. That first smell when you walk in just can't be matched."

I sighed. "Thanks for suggesting this. I wanted to come all summer but didn't have the time."

"I know. But sometimes you need to make the time for things you enjoy. Nothing relaxes me like this place." She frowned. "And it has nothing to do with Cedric Benoit, as much as I love him and his band."

"I'm sorry you get teased so much about that."

She shook her head. "They don't mean anything. It's all in fun."

Bless her forgiving, loving heart.

We walked quickly through the large store, which was actually the gateway to the park itself. I enjoyed browsing through the Silver Dollar City merchandise when I had the time, but we'd have to skip it today.

We exclaimed over the Christmas trees in Christmas Hollow and stopped at several open shops along the way, examining homemade candles, trinkets, and confections.

Nostalgia washed over me as I smelled popcorn when we drew near to the kettle-corn stand. Benjamin's favorite. I bought a bag to take home for him.

We walked over the bridge with the sound of a ghost rider, and further on enjoyed a waterwheel, turning in the stream.

As we turned the corner by the Dockside Theater where The Cajun Connection performed, my mouth watered at the aroma of BBQ beef and pork. The open café across from the theater drew us, and we lunched on BBQ sandwiches.

My eyes closed as I took the first delicious bite. "Yummy."

Miss Georgina giggled. "Me, too."

I glanced across the rustic wooden table. "Do you have any idea what's going on with Miss Jane?" I asked.

She darted a quick glance at me and swallowed. "What do you mean?"

"Now Miss Georgina, come on. You know very well what I mean." I grinned. "First of all, Miss Jane never passes up an opportunity to go to Springfield. And she blushed rather obviously when she spoke of her lunch date."

Miss Georgina waved a napkin in front of her face. I should have felt guilty, but since the seniors insisted on making my business theirs, it didn't bother me a bit to dig Miss Jane's secret from Miss Georgina's head.

"Oh, all right. I'll tell you." She cast an accusing glance at me as if I were forcing the information out of her. "Jane has been talking to Harvey Samson."

"The bakery guy?"

"Yes, he's the owner of Samson's Bakery. Inherited it from his father years ago."

"Is he a nice man?" The only thing I knew about him was that his donuts were wonderful. When they were fresh.

"Of course he's nice. Jane wouldn't be talking to him otherwise." She frowned. "And don't get any ideas. They are good friends, like Martin and me. That's all."

I nodded. "Okay. It's nice to have friends."

I bit into my sandwich and waited. I could see Miss Georgina had something right on the tip of her tongue. If I was patient, she'd blurt it out.

Pink washed over her face. "I've accepted a date to the movies and dinner with Martin. Don't you think a double date with Jane and Harvey would be fun?"

I coughed to cover the laugh that exploded from my throat. "Yes, ma'am. Benjamin and I double date with Phoebe and Corky a lot."

She nodded. "Exactly."

We talked about other possible places they could go for their double date while we finished our lunch, then headed across to the Dockside just as the music started.

I sat entranced during the show, as I always did. Miss Georgina wasn't the only one of our gang who enjoyed The Cajun Connection. I missed some of the former members of the band who had moved on to other things, but as long as Cedric was around—with his "bring down the house" voice, great Cajun music, and that magical accordion—I'd be a fan forever.

We made it to Johannsen's office at two o'clock sharp. I introduced Miss Georgina before we were seated.

Professor peered over the top of his half-lens glasses at me for a moment before he spoke. "Miss Storm, have you any idea what you have in your possession?"

"I have some suspicions, that's all. Why don't you tell me?"

"I'm not exactly sure. But these documents would appear to indicate smuggling activities during and shortly after World War II. Does that surprise you?"

"No, sir. Not really."

He looked at me for a moment, then took a deep breath. "Very well. Whatever you know about this, if anything, you've apparently decided not to share with me. And that's within your rights of course. I have a special interest in anything related to Germany during this time period. You see, I'm Jewish, and my parents emigrated from that country in the thirties.

I took the envelope he held across to me. "I see. Professor Johannsen, I promise if I find a story associated with these papers that I feel would be of interest to you, I'll share it. But I'll tell you this much now—the documents might very well lead to a crime against your people. And if it's possible to bring even one of the perpetrators to justice, that has to come before personal considerations."

He smiled. "On that, we are in agreement. Thank you for your promise."

"And thank you for translating. How much is your fee, by the way?"

"For this? Nothing. Find the criminals, if they still live. That will be more than enough payment."

I hesitated a moment, then reached into the envelope. Rifling through, I took out the ones that were in German and handed them back to him. "Here, I have another copy of these. And the translation is what I really need anyway."

Almost reverently, he reached for the documents. "Miss Storm, I don't know how to thank you."

"No need." I shook his hand, and Miss Georgina and I left his office.

We drove back to Cedar Chapel in silence, each lost in our own thoughts. At least I was. I suspected Miss Georgina was dozing.

We got back to the lodge around three thirty. The seniors' vehicles were in the garage.

"Let's wait until after dinner to get everyone together in the parlor. Then we'll look at these papers together."

If Miss Aggie was still missing, I'd have torn into them before we left Springfield, on the slim chance there might be a lead. But now that she was safe and sound, I wanted all the seniors to share the moment.

I locked the envelope in the file cabinet in my office, then went upstairs to straighten my room. I'd only had time to do a quick run through the guests' rooms before we'd left this morning, so mine had been ignored. Most of the seniors did their own light housework, but I still tried to do a quick check every day.

The phone rang. "Cedar Lodge."

"Hi, honey." Benjamin's voice was tinged with regret. "I'm sorry. I won't be able to come to dinner after all."

"Oh Benjamin."

"I know, honey. But I have too much work piled up."

"Humph. Didn't your wonderful secretary do anything while you were away?"

"Funny thing. They said she hasn't been here since I've been gone. Hasn't even called."

"Maybe she only wants to work when you're around."

"Now Vickie. Don't start up."

I laughed. "Just kidding. Maybe, with her mother gone, I'd better check on her in the morning, in case she's sick."

"That'd be nice of you."

"Will do. Good night, Ben."

I made my bed and did a quick cleanup in the bathroom, then sat in Grandma's rocker and picked up my Bible. I'd been so busy I'd gotten several days behind in my daily reading. I started with a passage in Numbers, which was the Old Testament reading from my guide. Halfway through, the old familiar guilt hit me. I realized I was trying to hurry through it.

"Lord, forgive me, and please show me that Numbers is a living part of Your Word, too."

I continued to the end of the passage, expecting a sudden revelation from God, but nothing jumped out at me. The New Testament reading was in Galatians, one of my favorite epistles. By the time I laid my Bible down on the table and spent a few minutes in prayer, it was time to go downstairs and help Miss Jane carry the food into the dining room.

ୡ

We gathered in the parlor after dinner. Frank started a fire to dispel the slight chill in the room. The smell of burning logs and crackle of the fire brought warmth, not only physically but emotionally.

I found myself almost reluctant to read the letters and other documents. What if, as it seemed possible, Jack Riley was implicated? How could I tell Phoebe? And would she ever forgive me for being the one to expose him?

I glanced around at my friends, Grandma and Grandpa's friends. How would I ever manage when they were gone?

I handed the envelope to Miss Evalina. "Would you read them, please?"

"Yes, of course." She gave me a sympathetic smile, and I knew she understood my sudden hesitancy. The dear woman probably knew me better than anyone, now that my grandparents were gone. Even better than Benjamin. She reached in and took out the documents.

"It seems your professor has grouped the documents according to their content. Why don't we start with the letters? Perhaps they will reveal the information you're looking for."

She took the first letter and read it aloud. A gasp from Miss Georgina spoke pretty well what I felt. The letters were written to Clyde from two different men in Germany. Apparently they worked for Jack Riley's import/export company. Each letter contained instructions concerning shipments of merchandise being smuggled to Pennington House. The earlier ones mentioned Miss Aggie's father. It became clear he had been receiving stolen property from Germany for several years before he died but thought he was dealing with legitimate merchandise. Forrest had caught on and brought Clyde in with him because of his knowledge of the language, as well as his almost idol worship of Forrest. They made a deal with the smugglers, who'd contacted those in charge in Germany. Clyde and Forrest became couriers, and after the elder Mr. Pennington died, they took over the illicit business.

"Victoria, you were wrong about Jack Riley. Listen to this." As she continued to read, it was apparent that Jack Riley knew nothing about the illegal actions of his employees, but they were sure he was starting to suspect something. There was a warning in two of the letters to be careful of Jack Riley.

Relief washed over me. I'd been wrong about Phoebe's uncle. I wished I hadn't wasted so much time suspecting him. Miss Evalina's voice was a little hoarse, so I asked her if she would like for me to continue.

Frank looked at me. "Here, why don't I take over?" When I nodded, he reached for the papers. "These appear to be bills of sale, as I mentioned before."

He scanned one, then the other. "Yeah, they're bills of sale and receipts for items purchased. Looks like they were copies of originals."

Martin sat on the edge of his chair and snorted. "Will you get on with it? What are they for?"

Ignoring his friend, Frank allowed his eyes to roam over the page.

"Frank." Miss Evalina got his attention.

"Nearly all jewels. A painting or two. Furs." He whistled. "Listen to this. One choker-type emerald necklace. A large heart-shaped emerald on a gold chain. Two emerald bracelets. One set of emerald earrings."

"The Pennington emeralds." Miss Georgina's awe-filled whisper was loud enough for all to hear.

I shivered. Who did they belong to? Where was their owner now? Visions of a gas chamber, stacked high with victims of the Holocaust, bombarded my mind. A pit, with men and boys standing at its edge, while black-clad men pointed rifles at their heads. Every picture I'd ever seen of these victims attacked my mind. The room started to spin.

"Victoria."

"Wh–what? Oh, sorry."

"It's all right, dear. I thought for a moment you were going to hyperventilate." Miss Evalina's calm voice soothed me.

Miss Georgina nodded, her silver curls bobbing. "That happened to me once. It was in the late forties when I first heard about the atrocities against the Jewish people. I almost passed out."

Miss Jane sighed. "No one talked about it back then. It was too horrible to think about, much less mention. I think the whole world tried to forget. It took a book by a man named Leon Uris to remind us that it had really happened."

"I wonder if the sheriff got his copies of these translated yet." Martin's practical voice brought me back to the present.

"I don't know. I guess I should find out and give these to him if he didn't."

"Let me call him," Frank said. "He won't yell at me."

I smiled, and Frank got up and went to the phone. A few minutes later he was back, grinning.

"He doesn't have them yet. You know how slow the department is. When I told him we had the translations, he about came unglued. I didn't tell him you were the one who'd had them, but he seemed to know anyway. Said he'd pick them up on his way to work in the morning and you'd better not let anything happen to them."

"In that case, I'll guard them with my life." I tried not to appear nervous, but I was quaking inside. I shouldn't have kept the copies. Maybe I'd better give the other copies to him, as well as the translation.

The phone rang, and I went to answer it.

Miss Aggie snapped, "Victoria, is that you?"

"Miss Aggie, it's so wonderful to hear your voice."

"It's very rude to answer the phone and not give your name."

"I'm sorry, ma'am. I won't do it again. When are you coming home? We miss you."

"Yes, so I hear. You've been putting up a fuss about me, too. I don't know why a lady can't go on a trip without everyone thinking she's kicked the bucket. I'm not a child, you know."

"I know, and I'm very sorry if I've offended you."

"I guess I'm not offended. I'll be home tomorrow. Make sure my rooms are aired out and clean."

As if I'd have allowed her rooms to get dirty. "Yes, Miss Aggie. I'll do that."

"Good night, then."

I giggled. Apparently her little adventure hadn't dampened her spirit. I relayed the message to the seniors. Then a thought crossed my mind. It was obvious to me that Jack Riley had suspected something was wrong at his place of business. Had he discovered the smuggling activities? I wondered if the sheriff would take him into his confidence and show him the letters and documents. If not, Mr. Riley might go on indefinitely trying to uncover the truth.

I went to my office and called him at Phoebe's. When he heard my voice, he apologized for canceling our meeting.

"That's quite all right. Phoebe explained about the business trip." He didn't need to know I thought he made it up.

"Oh good. Perhaps we could make it another time."

"Actually, I thought it would be nice if you came to dinner sometime soon."

"I'd be delighted. Name the day." He chuckled. "My niece is an excellent cook but tends to repeat the same menu over and over again," he whispered.

I laughed. "How about Saturday night?"

"I'd be delighted." He sounded like he meant it.

"Mr. Riley, I need to tell you something." I swallowed.

"Yes, what is it?"

"I came across some documents and letters written in German and had them translated. Some of them made mention of you. The sheriff is going to pick them up in the morning and take them to his office. I thought perhaps you'd like to see them."

CHAPTER ⚏ NINETEEN

A sense of foreboding fell on me as I polished the floor in the great hall. I tried to shake it off by blaming it on the darkness that hung ominous and threatening over the lodge. The storm had hit around 4:00 a.m. and had continued sporadically throughout the morning and early afternoon. I started as the grandfather clock chimed. Then once more. Two o'clock already? I backed out through the door, into the foyer and stood up. A long-ago memory surfaced, and I laughed. I'd decided to surprise Grandma by waxing the great hall while she was out shopping. When I realized I'd waxed myself right into the corner by the bay window, I'd hopped onto the window seat and spent the rest of the afternoon reading *The Password to Larkspur Lane*, which I'd left on the window cushion the day before. My favorite Nancy Drew book in those days. I still had the collection, inherited from Grandma. Maybe, someday, I'd take another trip down Larkspur Lane.

A loud clap of thunder reverberated through the house.

The weather forecaster had warned of tornadoes in the area, so the seniors had decided not to brave the elements. They'd spent most of the day in the rec room, watching movies and playing dominoes.

I decided I might as well do the foyer since I was stuck in the house, but I'd need more wax.

As I passed through the kitchen on my way to the basement, Mabel sighed.

I nodded. "I know. The weather is awful. You probably should have stayed home."

"If I'd heard about the tornado watch, I probably would have. But no use crying over spilt milk."

I went down the steps to the basement and grabbed more wax and buffing cloths. I should probably get an electric buffer, but Grandma had always done the waxing on her knees, so it was good enough for me. Buster whined from his pallet in the corner.

"What's the matter? Are you lonely down here?"

He came toward me, tail wagging, and rubbed his head against my leg. I reached down and scratched his ear. "Sorry, boy, I have more floors to do. Maybe later."

He lumbered back to his blanket and lay down.

Miss Jane was in the kitchen preparing a tea tray. She looked up as I came through the door. "Georgina and I decided to have a cup of tea. I have a feeling you could use one, too."

Mabel grumbled. "I told her I'd make it."

"But you said you need to go to the store before the storm hits again."

"I have time to make a pot of tea," Mabel retorted.

I rolled my eyes. Miss Jane had done a lot of the cooking after Corky left and before Mabel showed up at the door.

And she still did a lot on Mabel's day off. Hence, she felt like the kitchen was her domain. Sometimes, the friendly rivalry approached a little too close to unfriendly.

Mabel turned to me. "If you don't need me for a while, I'll go on to the store. I should be back before Sarah gets here, but if I'm not, you can make her wait in the kitchen."

I smiled. "Or she can wait in the parlor and visit with us until you get back."

She nodded and reached for her coat.

Miss Jane cleared her throat. "You are so right about me needing a cup of tea, Miss Jane. Where are the others?"

"Eva and Frank went upstairs. Martin's snoring on the rec room sofa. Between his snoring and the shoot 'em up he was watching, Georgina and I decided to have our tea in the parlor."

I chuckled. "I don't blame you. Here, let me take that tray."

I followed her into the parlor and put the tray on the coffee table.

Miss Jane picked up her cup. "Did I hear Buster whining?"

"Yes, I guess he thinks he's in trouble because I won't let him come upstairs."

Miss Georgina giggled. "Remember the day we brought Buster home?"

I gave a short laugh. "How could I forget? His filthy paws landed on my chest, nearly knocking me over. I seem to recall it took you and Miss Jane both to get him off me."

Miss Jane nodded. "Then Corky found the blood on Buster. If only we'd known he'd been with Aggie, maybe he could have led us to her that very day."

I wasn't in the mood to travel down that memory lane. "Yes, but we found her anyway. And all's well that ends well, as they say." And, thank the Lord, Miss Aggie was well this time, too.

Miss Georgina sighed. "I wonder what time she'll be home."

To be honest, I'd expected her before now. "Don't worry. She'll be here."

Lightning flashed through the room, and thunder boomed. A downpour of rain beat against the roof and windows. There was loud pounding on the front door, followed by the ring of the doorbell.

I ran to open the door before whomever it was got drenched. A raincoat-clad figure, hat pushed down low, shoved past me and yanked a gun from somewhere, shaking it in my face.

"Where are the documents?" The shrill words pierced through me as I realized who stood there.

"Christiana? What are you doing?"

She laughed. "What does it look like I'm doing? I'm pointing a gun at your face, and if you don't get those documents, I'll blow your head off."

"What documents?" Perhaps I could stall until I came up with an idea of what to do.

"Don't play games with me, Victoria Storm. I know my mother brought the documents to you before she left town. And there must be something about the treasure in them. I haven't searched this long to let someone else have them."

Realization hit me. "You're the one who shot at us at Pennington House?"

I heard the kitchen door close softly.

Christiana started. "What was that noise?"

"What? The thunder?" Was Mabel back so soon? My heart jumped. Or. . .was it already time for Sarah to be here? *Please, God, keep them both away.*

"Victoria, who was. . ." Miss Georgina stood in the parlor door with her mouth hanging open.

Christiana, her eyes wild, waved the gun at me. "Get in there. Who else is here?"

I stepped over to Miss Georgina, took her arm, and walked with her into the parlor. Miss Jane stood in the middle of the room, eyes wide.

The three of us sat on the sofa against the wall while Christiana stood in front of us with the gun.

"Now," she shouted, "I want those documents. They belonged to my grandfather, and they're mine."

"I'm sorry. I turned them over to the sheriff a couple of days ago."

"Don't give me that. I heard you talking to my mother about the sheriff. You don't like him, and you wouldn't have given them to him."

At this moment, the sheriff would be my best friend, if he showed up. But that wasn't likely to happen. My heart froze. Miss Aggie. What if she came in while Christiana was holding them at gunpoint? Would the girl shoot her? For that matter, she might fire on any or all of them at any time. I prayed Frank, Miss Evalina, and Martin would remain asleep.

"Christiana, while it's true the sheriff and I don't always get along, he's still the law around here, and I did give him the documents. I couldn't read them anyway because they were in German."

The girl's lips trembled, and for the first time, uncertainty filled her eyes. Then in a split second, rage filled her eyes. "You'd better not be lying to me."

"You can call him if you like." I tried to sound calm, while inwardly my stomach churned and my heart pounded.

Her hands began to shake, and I feared the gun might go off accidentally. Could I risk trying to knock it from her hands?

Over her shoulder, I saw Martin creep up to the door with a heavy vase in his hands. *No, no, Martin. If she hears you, she'll shoot.*

He drew closer and closer. He raised the vase above his head. His sharp intake of breath was so loud I heard it from the sofa. Christiana whirled around. I launched myself at her, knocking her to the floor.

She screamed, and the gun went off. I grabbed at her hand, trying to get a grip on the gun. My fingers wrapped around her wrist, and I squeezed. Martin grabbed the gun as it dropped from her hand.

She screamed again. "I'll kill you! I'll kill you!"

Martin aimed the pistol at her. "Young'un, you don't have the gun anymore. How are you gonna kill anyone?"

"Okay, I'll take over from here." Sheriff Turner and Deputy Lewis charged through the door, their sidearms drawn. Miss Aggie thundered past them and threw her arms around Miss Jane, then Miss Georgina.

Jack Riley stood in the doorway, but Benjamin shoved his way past him and hurried to take me in his arms.

"Are you all right?" His eyes scanned me from top to toe, searching for injuries.

"I'm fine, Ben. Except for my nerves. But why did you all get here at just the right time?"

Sarah's tiny form slipped around Mr. Riley. "Me and Miss Aggie called them." She stood in front of me, her thumbs in her jeans pockets. "I saw someone push you and shove their way in the door when I was walking from the bus, so I sneaked in the kitchen and listened. Then I ran out the back door just as Miss Aggie pulled up. I didn't know who she was, but I ran over to the car."

Miss Aggie nodded and looked at Sarah with admiration shining from her eyes. "The child was shaking so hard I could barely make out what she was saying, but she's a very brave and determined little girl."

Sarah giggled. "Yeah, I was shaking pretty good, but then I told her what I saw and heard. She called the sheriff, and we sat in the car until he got here. I wanted to come back in to make sure you were okay, but Miss Aggie wouldn't let me."

She rocked back and forth from heel to toe, her eyes shining. "Did I save you?"

I reached for her, and she came close and let me hug her. "Sarah Carey, you did indeed save me. You're my hero."

We stood together and watched as the sheriff snapped handcuffs on Christiana and took her away.

ભ

A charge of excitement ran through the lighted parlor. We'd called in for pizza, since the meat loaf Mable had prepared wouldn't have been enough for everyone. After we'd eaten, we went into the parlor. The seniors stared at Jack Riley expectantly. Benjamin and I sat on one of the love seats, leaning forward so we wouldn't miss a word. Was the man who'd been the focus of my suspicions for so long going to reveal all the secrets he'd held through the years? And if so, would the strands of mystery surrounding Pennington House finally become unraveled?

He leaned forward, his hands pressing against his clenched lips. He drew a deep breath and sat up straighter. "It's hard to know where to begin. This happened so long ago."

No one spoke or hardly seemed to breathe.

"You see, all I ever wanted was to build the business and take care of my family. Then, when Hitler began his insane vendetta against the Jewish people, my focus was on helping as many as possible. Through my connections in England and the United States, I was able to transfer a great deal of money and valuables for some. But when things got worse and people began to disappear, I knew I needed to concentrate on getting as many people out of the country as possible. Most left Germany with only the clothing on their backs.

"I still wanted to help with their assets, so I chose two of my employees, Frederick Heffner and Thomas Schmidt. Men who had been with me for a number of years. I taught them how to move the funds and property."

He coughed and cleared his throat. I picked up a pitcher of water and filled his glass.

He drank deeply and thanked me.

"I'm not sure when they decided to smuggle the goods for personal gain. I do know, in the beginning, legitimate transfers were made. After the war I began to suspect something dishonest was going on. In the autumn of 1950, I found evidence. When Heffner and Schmidt discovered I was on to them, they disappeared. I'm quite sure they had prepared ahead of time for just such a possibility.

"I discovered bills of sale and other papers itemizing some of the valuables they'd stolen."

I leaned forward. "Were the men ever apprehended?"

"No. I'm sorry to say, in spite of my attempts, they were never brought to justice. I recently discovered that Schmidt died of cancer in a hospital in Wales. I've no idea what happened to Heffner. He simply disappeared.

"For a number of years I turned my attention to finding the stolen goods and doing my best to return them to their rightful owners or their families. I've had some success, although too often the trail ended in the records of some concentration camp.

"I was especially interested in a group of emeralds taken from a very wealthy family in Berlin. I managed to find two descendants. A young brother and sister. They'd been living in a French orphanage for several years, since their parents died in an automobile accident."

Miss Aggie sat up straight. "So this is why you wished to find the rumored Pennington emeralds?"

He sent her an apologetic smile. "Yes, I'm afraid so. The recent documents that Miss Storm turned over to the sheriff confirmed that the emeralds were indeed in the hands of Clyde Foster and your brother."

Miss Aggie whirled and faced me. "What documents?"

I told her about the translations, and she nodded, smiling, not seeming in the least bit surprised. I would have expected some excitement at finally having proof that the jewels existed.

Mr. Riley nodded. "So, the jewels were at Pennington. At least at one time. But we'll probably never know who has them now, if anyone does."

Miss Aggie's cheek twitched, then a smile curved her lips. "Don't be too sure. I haven't been on a sightseeing trip, you know."

I coughed, spattering hot tea all over my lap.

Miss Aggie frowned. "Be careful, Victoria. You're so messy sometimes."

"Excuse me, Miss Aggie. I didn't exactly do it on purpose." I narrowed my eyes. "Do you have something to tell us?"

She grinned. "As a matter of fact, I do."

We waited while she looked around at her roomful of friends, an expression of glee on her face. "You know, you aren't the only ones who can investigate."

Frank, a little miffed that he and Miss Evalina had missed all the afternoon excitement, emitted an impatient *whoosh* of air. "Would you get on with it, Aggie?"

"Okay." Her voice sounded chipper. "I left the car in the parking lot deliberately, to throw anyone off the scent who might be following me."

Martin rolled his eyes and snorted.

"Don't you snort at me, Martin Downey. That's the way the detectives do it, you know. She frowned. "But I didn't know I'd left my cell phone, and the bracelet must have broken and slipped off when I got out of the car."

Miss Georgina threw her friend a confused look. "But Aggie, who was tailing you?"

"I don't know. But someone could have been. Whoever killed Clyde, maybe."

I had my own idea about that but kept it to myself.

Miss Aggie shifted in her chair. "You see, I'd suddenly decided it would be a good thing to go through Forrest's personal items. Simon kept them stored in his attic. Of course, he'd looked through them after Forrest's death, but since he had no idea he needed to search for evidence of a crime, he could easily have missed something."

Seeing her point, I nodded. "But your nephew and his wife were out of town."

"Exactly. I could have called him, but then I'd have had to explain what I was looking for. And to be honest, I didn't know. And I didn't want to tell Simon I suspected his father of being a crook."

I hadn't thought of that aspect.

"Go on, Aggie." Miss Jane's eyes were bright with excitement and maybe a bit of envy. This sort of thing was right up her alley.

Miss Aggie leaned toward Miss Jane, and I could almost picture them when they were girlhood best friends, tilting their heads together over their teenage secrets.

"I took the bus to Jefferson City and stored my suitcase in one of the lockers. Then I jumped in a cab and went to Simon's house. I didn't have a key, so I had to break a window to get in, but it was easy. Simon really needs to put in a security system, and I told him so, too. I went to the attic and started going through boxes and trunks. But there were so many, and it was getting late. I retrieved my suitcase and got me a hotel room for the night. I didn't want to stay anywhere nice, because whoever was tailing me would be sure to watch those places, so I went and got me a room in a dinky downtown hotel. I changed hotels every night, just in case, and stored my suitcase in the locker in the daytime." She glanced around, her eyes sparkling. "It's the most fun I've had in years."

"But Aggie," Miss Evalina said. "When the police found your suitcase, there was blood on some of your clothing. What happened?"

Miss Aggie appeared surprised for a minute, then laughed. "Oh. So that's why everyone thought I was dead. I broke my perfume bottle when I got out of my car at the airport. When I picked it up, I cut my hand. Look." She held her hand up. "It's still not all the way healed."

We stared at the deep scratch on her finger that had caused us so much grief and worry.

"I'm really sorry you were all so worried. I didn't know you'd find out that Simon was away. I thought if you called and no one answered you'd think we were out somewhere." She looked thoughtful. "I should have realized one of the kids would be going over to get their mail and stuff."

I smiled and, reaching over, patted her hand. "It's okay, Miss Aggie. You didn't know. So, did you turn up anything interesting in Forrest's things?"

Her lips tilted in a slow smile. She reached into her pocket and pulled out a yellowed sheet of paper, which she proceeded to unfold.

"This," she said, "is the map that will lead us to the Pennington jewels."

CHAPTER ⛩ TWENTY

Miss Aggie insisted on trudging the mile and a half to the cave entrance rather than go into the house through the secret room. After all, she didn't want to spoil our surprise before Pennington House's official opening day. So with the men loaded down with shovels and a pickax, we started off.

The storm had stopped, but a fine drizzle hit any uncovered skin it could find, and my slacks were drenched.

"I don't know why we can't take Benjamin's truck," Frank complained. "I don't like this at all."

Miss Aggie grabbed Corky's sleeve and stopped, whirling around to shine her flashlight in Frank's face. "I told you I don't want ruts on the lawn. And if we take the back road, we'll have to crawl through a barbed-wire fence."

Frank scowled. "I'm glad Evie stayed behind. At least she won't get sick, even if everyone else does."

"Hogwash, Frank Cordell," Miss Jane retorted. "Eva only stayed behind because she didn't want you to worry. She'd much rather be here with the rest of us."

At that, a sheepish look crossed Frank's face. "For crying out loud, Aggie, will you get that light out of my face?"

She turned the flashlight, and she and Corky started again, leading the way with Jack Riley and Frank close behind. We all knew the way to the storage cave, but she insisted. After all, it was her property and her map. And I wouldn't have had it any other way. I couldn't wait to see her face, if the jewels truly were where the map indicated. Of course, if they weren't. . .well, that didn't bear pondering. Because if they weren't there, then someone had already removed the jewels, and we'd never find them.

In front of me, Miss Georgina tripped, and Martin took her arm to steady her. Benjamin walked between Miss Jane and me, and I held tightly to his arm. I had a hunch Miss Jane held on tight, too.

Benjamin had suggested we clue the sheriff in, but Miss Aggie was adamant that it was none of his business. She intended to turn the jewels, if there were any, over to Jack, so he could attempt to get them to the owners or their descendants. If that wasn't possible, they would be donated to the state of Israel.

I couldn't get the two orphans out of my mind. I prayed the emeralds would be where Forrest's map indicated.

"There." Miss Aggie pointed to a marked tree. "The cave opening is behind these bushes."

Corky and Benjamin held branches back while the rest of us passed through. The cave entrance yawned before us. I knew there was a drop into the cave.

Benjamin jumped down. "Corky, if you'll help the ladies, I'll make sure they don't fall."

One by one, Corky lowered us into Benjamin's strong hands.

When he set me down, I glanced around. The cave looked just the same as it had the last time we'd been here. That's when we'd discovered it had been used as a holding area for the contraband that had been passed through the tunnel on tracks to the secret office.

Miss Aggie turned her flashlight toward the corner nearest the tunnel entrance, then stepped over and looked downward. She turned. Corky had jumped down into the cave, and she waved him over.

"This should be the spot." She took a deep breath. "I need to sit down. I feel a little faint."

Corky put his arm around her protectively while Jack brought a wooden box for her to sit on. I handed her a bottle of water from my backpack. She drank, then replaced the lid, nodding to Corky.

Benjamin and Corky took turns digging in the red-dirt floor of the cave, occasionally using the pickax to break up extremely hard-packed clay. Jack, Frank, and Martin directed beams of light from their flashlights.

Finally, the sound of metal on metal rang through the cave. Miss Aggie jumped up. "You've found it!"

"Now wait a minute, Aunt Aggie. We don't know for sure."

Corky bent down and began to dig with his hands, brushing dirt aside as he went. "There's something here, all right. Benjamin, I need a hand. It's wedged in pretty deep."

Tugging and grunting, they heaved a heavy iron box out of the hole and set it on the ground in front of Miss Aggie. Silence hung over the cave. I knew I couldn't speak if I tried. Was this the famous buried treasure? The Pennington jewels found, at last?

Miss Aggie looked at the heavy padlock. "How will we get that thing off?"

Corky put his hand on her shoulder. "Let's take it to the house, Aunt Aggie."

"No, no. I don't want anyone to see the house yet. We'll have to take it to the lodge."

With the heavy box between Benjamin and Corky, we trudged back to the vehicles, the going a lot slower this time.

By the time they piled into Benjamin's Avalanche and Corky's SUV, the seniors were exhausted from the walk and the excitement. I had to admit, I was winded myself. I scooted in next to Benjamin, and Miss Jane got in beside me. We both leaned back and sighed.

Benjamin laughed. "You sounded exactly the same."

Miss Jane smiled. "That's because Victoria and I are kindred spirits."

"We are, indeed. Friends and companions in adventures unimaginable."

"Yes, and many more in the future."

I laughed. "But maybe we could wait awhile and let this adventure settle a little."

When we got back to the lodge, I started the coffeemaker and put the teapot on, while Corky and Benjamin carried the heavy box down the outside basement steps. They'd knocked most of the dirt off, but I wasn't taking any chances.

Frank headed up the stairs. "Don't open it yet. Let me get Evie first."

Buster nosed around the box, and I shoved him back.

"What do you need to break the lock? Will a hammer do?"

Corky pursed his lips and looked thoughtful. "It might.

The hinge looks pretty rusty."

Frank and Miss Evalina came down the steps. Benjamin looked inside my toolbox and found the heaviest hammer I had. Three blows later, the padlock lay on the floor

Corky put his hand on Miss Aggie's back and gave her a gentle shove. "Go ahead, Aunt Aggie. Do the honors."

She walked forward and fumbled with the hasp. She gave a little tug, but nothing happened. Turning to Jack Riley, she said, "Will you open it, Jack? After all, you've been searching a long time."

He stepped forward. "Are you sure?"

"Yes, I'm sure. Otherwise I wouldn't have said it. Open the box."

We all leaned forward with bated breath as Jack gave a tug and yanked the lid up.

A cloth of some sort covered whatever was inside. Jack smiled at Miss Aggie and motioned for her to remove it.

I'll never forget my first glimpse of the contents of that rusty iron box.

A divided tray displayed what appeared to be diamonds, of every size and shape. One compartment held a matched set of necklace, earrings, and bracelet. Another contained three brooches. And the next, a diamond stickpin and cuff links.

At Jack Riley's intake of breath, I looked at him. Tears were in his eyes. "I recognize all of these."

Corky lifted the tray, revealing another underneath. Loose stones, which appeared to have been removed from settings, lay in each compartment.

Jack Riley's lips tightened, as did the muscles in his face. An expression of agony crossed his features. "Let's see the next one." His voice was hoarse.

The emeralds rested on what might have once been a white velvet lining. Even now, after being locked away for so many years, the stones winked and sparkled.

Miss Aggie lifted the jewels out one by one and held them in her hand. She slipped the bracelet on her wrist, then held the heart-shaped necklace up to her throat. She put one earring on her ear, turning the little wheel in back until it fit. I watched, entranced, as she closed her eyes for a moment. Then one by one, she carefully placed the jewels back in the trays.

She smiled at Mr. Riley. "There, now I've worn them. Please try to put them into the hands of their rightful owners."

With a tear in the corner of her eye, she climbed the steps and disappeared into the kitchen.

I glanced around. "You know what I can't understand. If Forrest had the map all these years, why didn't he retrieve the jewels?"

Mr. Riley nodded. "A very interesting question, Miss Storm. Perhaps Aggie has the answer and will share it with us. If not, then we'll likely never know."

∞

The next morning we all met at the courthouse. The sheriff really needed a bigger office. How did he expect us all to squeeze in there? Somehow we'd managed, though. Tom had brought chairs, and we all sat in a double semicircle around Sheriff Turner's desk.

He frowned. "I don't know why everyone needs to be here. I had business with Riley about jewels found on the Pennington property and with Victoria about the break-in at the lodge."

I almost snorted but controlled myself. I didn't want to sound like Martin. "Sheriff, you know very well what we've all been through because of these jewels. And anything that happens at the lodge is of concern to all of us."

"All right, all right. Jack Riley's story checks out, and the jewels match the ones stolen from Germany and other countries in Europe. I'm prepared to sign them over to him and let him continue his work.

"Now for the other matter." He fired a look at me. "You could have been killed. You should never let a stranger into your house."

"She wasn't a stranger."

"But you didn't know that. As it turns out, you'd have been better off if it had been a stranger." He huffed and shook his head. "Christiana Baker admitted to coming here to harass her grandfather into revealing where the jewels were hidden."

Miss Jane said, "But how did she know about them in the first place?"

"Seems her grandmother, Clyde's ex-wife, told Laura Baker the rumored story of the lost jewels and her suspicions that Clyde had them stashed somewhere. Christiana got it into her head to get them from her grandfather. So she came here secretly. She says they argued, and as he turned to walk away from her, he tripped, hitting his head on the doorstop. She got scared and ran."

Benjamin, his reporter antennae up, leaned forward. "Do you think she's telling the truth?"

Sheriff Turner scratched his head. "Yeah. Yeah, I do. She took a lie detector test and passed it. The death was accidental.

Too bad she has all those other charges against her. I think she must have gone a bit crazy."

"Yes." Miss Aggie's voice sounded faraway. "Jewels sometimes do that to a person."

"She's out on bail. Her mother hired some fancy lawyer. He'll probably get her off. I'll be surprised if she serves any time at all."

I shivered at the thought of Christiana's wild eyes as she waved the loaded gun at us. "If you're right, I hope they at least get her help. She obviously has a mental problem."

Our business seemed to be over, so we left. Jack would carry the jewels with him when he left in a few days. In the meantime, they were locked safely in the bank.

Benjamin needed to get his article written on the jewels, so he headed back to the *Gazette*, while Corky headed out to Pennington House.

Frank and Miss Evalina got into their truck and left for the center, and Miss Aggie, who'd finally gotten her Lexus back and was pretty well glued to it, followed the rest of us home.

Miss Jane glanced at her watch. "It's only nine thirty. We might as well go on to the center."

Miss Georgina glanced at me, her eyes filled with mirth, and winked. "Oh Jane, why don't we stay home today and play cards? I'm not in the mood for the center."

"Hah! I'm going whether you do or not. I have other friends, too, you know." She stopped and stared at my face, then glanced back at Miss Georgina. She took a deep breath, then smiled. "You're teasing me."

I threw a grin her way. "Turnabout's fair play."

She smiled. "You're right. I've given her a hard time about Martin, not to mention the handsome Cedric."

Martin snorted. "She don't care nothing about that Cajun."

"Don't you think I know that? But he's still handsome." Miss Jane threw him a glare, then continued. "Oh, all right. I am sort of seeing someone."

"Yes," Miss Georgina chimed in. "We're double-dating Saturday afternoon. Guess where we're going?"

"Hmm." I pretended to be deep in thought. "Lunch and a matinee?"

"No," she chortled. "We're going to Silver Dollar City. Harvey's never been there. Can you believe it?"

I put a serious look on my face and glanced at Miss Jane. "You'll be opening a whole new world to him. He's lucky he met you."

"Don't be silly. I've known him at least twenty years."

Laughing, I pulled into the garage. The three of them immediately got into Miss Jane's Cadillac and left.

Miss Aggie pulled in beside the van and got out.

"Aren't you going to Pennington House today, Miss Aggie?"

"Maybe later." She bit her lip. "Victoria, I need to talk to you about something."

"Okay, let me check on Buster, and then I'll join you in the parlor."

She nodded and preceded me into the house. After she'd left the kitchen, I took Buster out of the basement and let him into the backyard.

Mabel glanced at me when I came back in. I could see

from the expression on her face she was about to burst from curiosity, so I told her everything that had transpired the night before and what we'd found out from the sheriff.

Wondering what Miss Aggie wanted to talk to me about, I went to the parlor. She sat on the sofa, fidgeting with a ball of yarn.

She tossed it into the yarn basket on the floor. "Sit by me over here, Victoria."

Curious about her apparent agitation, I sat beside her. "Miss Aggie, is something wrong? You look worried."

She bit her lip. "I have a confession to make."

I almost groaned out loud. What had she done now? "A confession? What is it?"

She picked up the ball of yarn again and began unwinding it. Whatever she'd done, or thought she'd done, she seemed to be in the throes of guilt over it.

"Promise you won't tell any of the others?"

"Of course, I'd never betray your confidence."

"You see, I've had the map all along." She darted a glance at me and quickly averted her eyes, staring fixedly at the yarn.

"What?" Surely she was teasing.

She nodded. "I found the map in Robert's things after his accident."

"Robert? You mean your husband?"

She nodded. "I knew he was up to something that night. That day, he'd gotten a call. He'd said he'd take it in his office. By that time in our marriage, I'd lost all my trust for him. I knew he was after my inheritance. I picked up the extension in the kitchen. He was talking to Forrest. They spoke of the emeralds. Forrest said he never should have trusted him. Robert laughed and said he'd moved the jewels to another location, and Forrest would never find them. Forrest threatened him, and Robert laughed and hung up. I've always thought Forrest had something to do with the brawl that started that night that led to Robert's death."

She took a deep breath and drank a sip of tea. "I was so frightened. I didn't know what Forrest would do. I found the map in Robert's safe. I knew it was the new location, because the notations on the map were in his handwriting.

"I found the location and covered it with a stone. It looked natural, so I was pretty sure no one would suspect anything was there.

"That's when Forrest started after me to sell the house to those men he knew. But I knew what they were after. So I closed up the house and moved to the house on the beach."

"So, Forrest dropped the subject?"

"Heavens, no. There were break-ins from time to time. But I didn't care. As long as he never found the jewels. You see, I thought they'd belonged to my father, and therefore to me."

"But why did you keep them hidden?" With her love of valuable jewels, this was beyond my understanding.

"Because, you see, I was afraid. I didn't want to part with them. But if Forrest had killed Robert, he'd come after me, if he knew I had them."

Okay, something else was bothering me.

"Why, then, did you pretend to find the map in Forrest's belongings?"

"Oh, I didn't pretend, dear. I hid it there myself several years ago so I wouldn't forget where the jewels were buried.

But after all the killings and other mayhem, I didn't want anyone to know. I felt responsible somehow. Then, when you began to suspect Jack of being a smuggler, it all became clear to me. I knew I couldn't keep the jewels if they rightfully belonged to someone else. I decided it was time to 'find' them."

She cut a glance at me. "Do you hate me?"

"Oh Miss Aggie." I put my arm around her and kissed her on her cheek. "Of course not. The killings and other crimes were never your fault. They were the fault of greedy men who had no consciences."

"But, I was greedy, too."

"No, it wasn't greed. It was your youthful love of pretty things. You never quite outgrew that, did you?"

She shook her head, and pity for her washed over me. But I knew it wasn't simply a love of pretty things with her. It was a desire to always have more than others, and at times that desire had evolved into a compulsion to obtain what belonged to someone else. Such as with Frank Cordell, who had always belonged to Miss Evalina. Miss Aggie had never quite outgrown that character flaw. That is, until now.

"You won't tell anyone?"

"No. It's none of their business. It'll be our secret forever."

Joy shone on her face. She'd found absolution.

EPILOGUE

The wine-colored stairs were like cushy velvet beneath my pearl white pumps. I stood at the top of the staircase and looked down the sweeping arc of steps. I could see the top of Dad's head as he waited below to offer his arm and escort me into the grand ballroom. Prisms hung from the chandeliers, casting brilliant dancing lights on the walls and ceiling of the massive foyer.

Phoebe had stood here the week before when she'd married Corky. Her wedding had been the very first in the newly opened Pennington House. But I didn't care. Today was my day. And no one had ever been this happy.

I drew in a deep breath of vanilla-scented air and stepped down. My heart pounded at the thought of Benjamin waiting for me in the ballroom. I'd be able to see him as soon as I stepped off the stairway. I took another step. Would he think I was beautiful? Of course he would. His eyes would mist, and he'd look at me adoringly as I walked toward him on my father's arm. My Benjamin.

I took another step. . . .

My brand-new cell phone shrilled. Now why had I put my phone in the pocket of my wedding gown? For that matter, why did my gown have a pocket?

"Victoria. Victoria." Miss Georgina's screech pierced my ear. "You have to come with me."

"Shhh, Miss Georgina. I'm getting married. Get off the phone please."

"No, no, you have to come with me, now. Aggie's gone missing again."

"Oh no, please, God." I took another step and stumbled, falling. . .falling. . .falling.

"Victoria."

I sat straight up, my heart hammering and my pajama top drenched with perspiration.

"Victoria." My mother's gentle whisper, drifting through my bedroom door, was nothing like the screeching voice of my nightmare. "Wake up, sweetheart."

Relief washed over me. For a moment, on waking, I'd thought the dream was reality. I jumped up and went to let Mom in.

She breezed in, her makeup done to perfection and her soft brown hair perfectly arranged.

She gave me a peck on the cheek. "Can you believe it's your wedding day?"

I grinned. "Yes, but just barely."

"Get dressed, dear. Your father is waiting to have breakfast with you."

"I don't think I can eat anything. My stomach feels a little queasy."

"That's only wedding-day nerves. You'll feel better after you've eaten." Mom's no-nonsense tone made it clear she'd not be crossed.

"Okay. I'll shower and be down in a minute. Tell Dad to go ahead and eat. He doesn't have to wait."

"He won't hear of it. Hurry down now." She breezed out

of the room in the same manner she'd breezed in. I could hear the lilt of her voice as she sailed down both flights of stairs. I knew she sailed down. That was Mom's way. I guessed she was greeting the seniors.

After I'd showered and dried my hair, I yanked on jeans and sweatshirt and headed for the door. Then I stopped, turned, and grabbed my cell phone from the nightstand. The phone was a gift from Miss Aggie. According to her, no woman should be without one. I stuffed it into my pocket and hurried down to the dining room.

Dad stood and took my hand as I came to the table. He had an amused expression on his face. "Mr. Downey has been telling me about his W. C. Fields collection. I think maybe we'll have to watch some of those before I leave."

"Now, Robert, don't be silly. You know very well we're leaving in the morning."

Dad frowned. "I thought I might stay in Cedar Chapel a few days."

She looked at him, brows raised. "What in the world for? Victoria will be on her honeymoon, remember?"

"Maybe I'll look up some of my old friends. A few must still be around."

"Suit yourself, dear. But I have to be in New York City the day after tomorrow for Helen Lake's Christmas bazaar. I promised."

An old familiar sadness gripped me, and my breaths quickened. *Stop it, Victoria. You're a grown woman. And your mother will never be what you want her to be.*

I reached for my water glass and took a deep drink. I had Jesus. And Benjamin. And the seniors. I'd be fine.

Mom drew a deep, noisy breath. "Or maybe I'll skip the bazaar."

I looked at her to see what she was up to.

She was smiling at Dad, and he appeared very pleased.

Mom had always hated Cedar Chapel. Was she mellowing out in her old age? Or, at least, older age. Fifty-three wasn't that old.

After breakfast Dad announced he'd be in the rec room watching TV with Martin.

Mom took me by the arm. "Let's go upstairs and have a mother-daughter talk."

I looked at her in astonishment. Surely, she didn't mean. . .

"Oh, close your mouth. That's not the kind of mother-daughter talk I meant."

I let out a *whoosh* of air. "That's a relief. I wasn't sure."

We settled in the sitting room. Mom in the recliner and me in the rocking chair.

Mom shook her head. "I can't believe you kept that old thing."

"It's Grandma's."

A shadow crossed her face. "You loved her very much, didn't you?"

I nodded and blinked back the tears that filled my eyes.

She sighed. "She was more your mother than I ever was."

I stared at her, mute. That was probably the most serious sentence I'd ever heard her utter.

As if she read my mind, she nodded. "I know I'm very superficial most of the time."

"I didn't say that, Mom. And I didn't think it either."

"Sweetheart, I'm so sorry I wasn't the kind of mother you needed."

I swallowed past the lump in my throat and opened my mouth, but no words came forth. I had no idea what to say.

"I was so young and self-centered when I married your father." She paused, and pain crossed her face. "When you were born, I had no idea how to be a mother, and I suppose I may have resented the fact that I was expected to stay home and give up all my interests to care for a child."

"Mom, it's all right. You don't have to do this."

"Yes, because I want you to know."

For the first time, I noticed tears spilling over onto her cheeks. I handed her a box of tissues, disturbed at her sudden self-chastisement.

"By the time I realized what I'd done to you, it was too late. When I tried to reach out to you, I found you no longer wanted my attention." She bit her lip. "You had your grandmother, and you didn't need me."

"Mom, please don't. It's all right. Yes, I missed you. I couldn't understand why you were always away. But I wasn't the only girl at boarding school who seldom saw her parents."

She squeezed her eyes tight, and I realized I'd said the wrong thing.

I reached over and took her hand.

She turned imploring eyes on me. "Victoria, in spite of what you might think, I have always loved you very much. I hope you'll believe that."

"I do now. And you'll never know what it means to me to hear you say it. I love you, too, Mom." I smiled and squeezed her hand. "Now, let's leave the past behind. I'm getting married in a couple of hours to the man I love with all my heart. And I have my mother here to straighten my veil."

"I'll be there for my grandchildren. I promise. Maybe not every week or even every month, but they'll know I love them." She smiled. "Now, let's get you ready for that wedding."

An hour later, Mom and Dad drove me to Pennington House. My wedding gown was waiting for me in a luxurious suite on the second floor. The wedding was a gift from my parents. The wedding location was a gift from Miss Aggie and Corky. They'd provided me with the most luxurious guest suite in the hotel. Phoebe, my matron of honor, was there ahead of me in her wine-colored gown.

She and Mom helped me into my dress and veil, and then Mom went downstairs to be seated.

Strains of Mozart announced the beginning of the procession. Phoebe gave me a hug and hurried downstairs to make her entrance.

A few minutes later, I stood at the top of the sweeping staircase. I stepped slowly down the stairs and placed my hand on my father's waiting arm. The pianist struck the bride's cue, and we stepped forward.

As we walked into the grand ballroom, my eyes met Benjamin's. What I saw there was pure adoration. I smiled as I walked toward him.

My best friend. My heart's desire. My Benjamin. Always and forever.